The Cotton-Pickers

Also by B. Traven
and published by Allison & Busby

The Kidnapped Saint

B. Traven

The Cotton-Pickers

ALLISON & BUSBY, LONDON

This edition published in Great Britain 1979
by Allison & Busby, Limited,
6a Noel Street, London W1V 3RB

ISBN 0 85031 284 1 (hardback)
ISBN 0 85031 285 X (paperback)

1000677778 T

Printed in Great Britain by A. Wheaton & Company Limited, Exeter

Song of the Cotton-Pickers

Cotton is worn by king and prince,
Millionaire and president,
But the lowly cotton-picker
Sweats to earn each bloody cent.
 Get going to the cotton field,
 The sun is moving up and up.
 Sling on your sack,
 Tighten your belt—
 Listen, the scales are turning.

Look at the food I get to eat—
Beans and chile, tortilla-bread—
And the scarecrow shirt I swiped,
Torn by bush and patched with shreds.
 Get going to the cotton field,
 The sun is moving on and on.
 Sling on your sack,
 Tighten your belt—
 Listen, are the scales begging?

Cotton sells at soaring prices,
But I ain't got a decent shoe.
My pants hang down in ragged threads,
Here and there my butt shows through.
 Get going to the cotton field,
 The sun climbs high too soon.
 Sling on your sack,
 Tighten your belt—
 Listen, are the scales bossing?

On my head a straw sombrero,
Kicked in when I got beat.
But I couldn't pick without it
Bending in the burning heat.
    Get going to the cotton field,
    The sun is aiming high.
    Sling on your sack,
    Tighten your belt—
    Hey, are the scales trembling?

I'm just a lousy vagabond,
See, that's the way they made me be,
And there's no cotton crop for you
Unless it's picked by bums like me.
    March!—in cotton-picking ranks
    Beneath the firing sun!
    Or fill your sacks with rocks—
    Hear, are the scales breaking?

Book One

1

    The train that had brought me to this forlorn-looking little place had just left and I was standing on the station platform looking around in search of someone who might be able to tell me what I so very urgently needed to know.

Everyone looked so utterly depressing. There were some peasants in white cottons of many washings walking about on the platform and sitting on the ground alongside. The women had their arms full of children and were surrounded by a dozen more holding on to their mothers' skirts, with expressions of fear and wonder written all over their young faces, which were covered with chalky dust.

While I was lost in examining the landscape, and trying to make up my mind whom to approach for the very much wanted information, I suddenly realized that someone had stopped abruptly close in front of me, his nose almost touching the point of mine. Instinctively I stepped back a few inches and saw it was a very tall and heavily built Negro, who was addressing me: "Mister, can you maybe tell me which direction to take to a nearby ranch owned by a farmer called Mr. Shine?"

"What do you want to see that Mr. Shine for?" I blurted out. In the same moment I regretted that explosion of mine. The sudden nearness of the fellow had caught me in the very midst of a hard thinking process intimately connected with the hopeless state of my present economic situation. And so as to have that giant black fellow thinking better of me and my character I added rapidly: "See here, friend, that Mr. Shine you mention is precisely the very same person I myself have come to this godforsaken village to see."

"Also because of cotton, Mister?" he asked.

"Also because of cotton, which I want to help him harvest, or let's more correctly call it, to pick."

We were still looking at each other uncertainly, obviously not knowing what else to say or to do, when up trotted rather haltingly a little Chinaman with a friendly grin all over his face (even both his ears seemed to grin). "Good molning, caballelos, gentlemen," he greeted us. "Can you pelhaps, kind paldon, tell me the way to——"

Here he stopped, fumbled in the breast pocket of his snow-white collarless shirt, pulled out a bit of notepaper, unfolded and handed it to us, and, never losing his bright grin, started to read the line scribbled on it: "Ixtli . . ."

"Stop," I halted him. "You might get a knot in your tongue if you go on trying to pronounce the name of that place. The name is Ixtlixochicuauhtepec, am I right or am I?"

"Pelfectly collect, señol, it's exactly the name."

"Well then," I said, "your problems will be solved now, because that's exactly the very place we also are headed for. So, friend, welcome. You may join us."

Ixtli . . . If only I had the faintest idea where that village, or ranchería, whatever it might be, could be found. To the north? To the south or west? Well now, let's see, there must be somewhere around this railroad depot somebody who knows where to find that place with such a tongue-twisting Aztec name.

The people loitering on the platform were Indios and Mestizos, except for another Negro. He was as black as the giant one by my side but a foot shorter and very lightly built. How long he had been standing there calculating our threesome I don't know, but when he caught my eye he approached us with a sure step.

"Mister," he said, "could you by any chance tell me the whereabouts of a Mr. Shine, a cotton farmer? They tol' me in Tampico he's lookin' for hands to help with his cotton crop and I'd find him near to this here railroad station."

"Well! His whereabouts is exactly what we'd like to know. We're also looking for that cotton farm. Come along with us."

"Thanks a lot, fellers. Glad to have company in this bush. Mighty happy to be accompanied in this part of the country, where you meet, I been tol', all sorts of wil' beasts, tigers, leopards."

We were now sort of an organized group for the long or short trip—we didn't know which. That was how matters stood when a man came up whom I judged to be a Mestizo from the way he was dressed. He had slung about his upper body a red, tattered, formless piece of coarse-wool blanket and he wore the customary white, sloppy wide-brimmed bast hat—or was it reed? His bronze-brown face was covered by a growth of beard. He was middle-aged, of medium build, slender but doubtless a man used to hard work. His beat-up dirty tennis shoes had once upon a time been white. I remembered I had seen this man on the train, traveling in the same car which I had chosen to come here.

Scrutinizing our little assembly, as if searching for someone among us whom he might perhaps know, he decided to put his question to me: "Buenos días, señor, are you perhaps Mr. Shine?"

"No," I said, "I'm not Mr. Shine, but I'm here to meet him somewhere in this neighborhood."

"Is this the place?" So saying he produced a scrap of muddy paper torn from a newspaper, on which was scribbled: Ixtlixochicuauhtepec.

"Yes, that's the place, amigo. We're going there; so if you wish to come along with us, bienvenido, you are invited."

"Nothing better could have happened to me. Muchas gracias, mil, mil gracias. I'll be only too grateful to be in your company. Again, many, many thanks." He bowed with the innate courtesy of a Mexican.

Then he turned slightly around, fingering his beard, undecided as to what to do or say next. Seeing him turn aside like that gave me the idea that we had better start going now and right away, or a dozen more people in need of a job might try to join us.

Sure enough, another Mexican came leisurely walking up. He was not a Mestizo like the previous one; this was a Mexican of pure Indian stock, dressed in very clean white cotton, for shoes the local huaraches—no socks, of course—and carrying over his shoulder a beautiful blanket in bright colors, a so-called sarape, as well as a small bundle rolled inside a reed mat. He just stood there looking at us, not saying a word.

"Need any help?" I asked in Spanish.

"Si, señor. Do you know the way to Ixtlixochicuauhtepec?" A true son of the land, he had no difficulty pronouncing the name of the place.

"No," I answered, "but I'm just about to find out. Keep close to us, if you wish; we're all going cotton-picking at six centavos a kilo. As soon as we find out which way to go to Mr. Shine's farm, we'll get started."

Get started! If only I knew which way to go.

The station meanwhile, ten minutes after the one train of the day had departed, had emptied and lay drowsy and deserted in the tropical heat, as only a station in this part of America can. The mail bag, which looked all bag and no mail, had already been carried off. The goods—a few cases of merchandise, two drums of kerosene, five rolls of barbed wire, a bag of sugar—were lying still unclaimed on the blistering hot platform.

The wooden shack where tickets were sold and luggage was weighed had been padlocked. The man responsible for the official duties had left the station before the last car had gone by. Even the little old Indian woman who, like her counterparts at all the village depots of the countryside, appeared at every train arrival with her reed basket containing tortillas and two bottles of cold coffee, even she was already a fair distance away, slipping through the tall grass toward home. She was always the last to leave the platform. Although she never sold anything, she came every day to meet the train. The coffee she brought to the station was probably the same for weeks on end. Evidently the travelers suspected this; otherwise they might have given the old woman a chance to earn something now and then, especially in that heat. But anyhow the ice water that was available on the trains free of charge put the old woman's cold coffee right out of business.

My five companions had seated themselves happily on the ground near the wooden shack—in the shade; though it must be admitted that, as the sun was standing vertically above us, it took a man of some experience to discover where the shade actually was.

Time did not matter to them; and since they knew that I wanted to go where they wanted to go they left the reconnaissance to me. Without formal election I had become the leader of our little group. They would go when I went, and not before; and they would follow me even if I took them to Argentina.

There was not a house to be seen anywhere near the station. Looking off in the direction taken by the last group of departing natives, whom I could see still making their way through the grass, I suggested to my companions that we follow them, with the idea that they might lead us into the town or direct us to it.

It didn't take us long to catch up with them. "Never heard of a farm or a place by that name, señor," they answered when I approached them. "But come along with us. Surely in the town someone will know the way."

We soon reached the village. The dwellings there were crude huts surrounded by banana plants and tall mango trees which, although never tended in these regions, bear great quantities of fruit. The little fields were sown with maize and beans well beyond the needs of the few people there.

It would have been quite pointless to go to one of these huts and ask the way to Ixtli. . . . If these people gave an answer at all, it would be an unreliable one. Not that they would deliberately mislead us, but out of sheer politeness they would want to give a pleasant answer and avoid the necessity of saying "I don't know."

Besides the huts, there were two wooden buildings in the village. In one of them, our friends pointed out, lived the stationmaster, of whom we should ask the way; the other was a poolroom.

I went to the stationmaster's house, but he did not know where Ixtli . . . was. He added politely that he had never heard of the place but, then, he'd only recently been transferred to this town. So I walked over to the poolroom, where I found an intelligent-looking man inside idly leaning against a pool table. He greeted my entrance with an inviting smile.

"Siento mucho, señor," he answered my question, "I'm awfully sorry to disappoint you, but despite my living here for the last five years I've never heard of that place. By all means it has a very uncommon name as far as our state is concerned. Now, señor, I don't want to appear impolite, but if you don't mind telling me what your business is at that village, if it is a village, that just might tickle my memory and give me a tip to that particular place among the many I know. You see, then I might be able to help you out in your trouble."

"Now here we come perhaps closer to a solution. I'm interested in cotton, so, then, it must be a place where cotton is grown."

He brightened up visibly, apparently relieved that he could help me. I had judged him from the first to be the good-neighbor type.

"Since you mention cotton, señor, I remember that about three years or so ago there arrived here one day a line of heavy trucks loaded to the top with bales of freshly harvested cotton, bringing it to this depot from where it would be taken by train to the nearest port. I understood it was to be loaded on ships and taken to Europe or one of those foreign countries with a crazy name. They all came from that direction."

With this he waved an arm vaguely, much as a huge bird would flap its wing as it tried to lift itself into the air. The direction indicated by his waving, rolling arm could have been to the north as well as to the west or the east. However, it indicated at least one direction which positively should not be taken.

"How far do you think it might be to that place where these people came from?"

"Far as I can remember these gringos saying, because you should know that they are all gringos holding those lands, they had left by six in the morning and when they arrived here it was noon. So you can figure out for yourself the distance, considering that there's no road and they surely had to cut their way through the bush with a machete—certainly not an easy way to travel. Not so unlikely a few traces of that road they cut might still be visible enough to follow."

"Gracias mil veces, señor," I broke out happily, "thank you a thousand times. You certainly did me a great favor at a moment when I felt as though the world were sinking under my feet." I shook his hands vehemently and did so joyfully.

"Now we're finally getting somewhere," I told myself over and over again, walking back to where I had left the group of hungry job-seekers, of whom I was the hungriest, to tell the truth.

We decided to leave right away and go as far as we could before sunset, after which it would be next to impossible to discover and follow the traces of the road that might still be there, as that good man in the poolroom had indicated.

2

   So off we marched in good enough spirits. The six
of us felt as happy in one another's company as
brothers who had unexpectedly met in some strange out-of-
the-way place after a long separation.

Above us the scorching tropical sun, about us the dense
impenetrable bush; the eternally virgin bush of the tropics
with its indefinable mystique, its fantastic secret animal life, its
dream-shaped, dream-colored plants, its unexplored treasure of
stone and metal.

But we were not explorers, nor were we gold or diamond
diggers. We were workers, and set more store on certain
earnings than on the uncertain promise of the millions that
may have been hidden in the bush around us, waiting to be
discovered.

We hiked through the wild unbroken bushland, sweating
under a tropical sun, without the faintest idea where and when
we would locate Mr. Shine's cotton plantation. It might be
fifty miles away, perhaps sixty. What if it were eighty or a
hundred miles? We simply had to find work.

We discovered a narrow path and marched forward in
single file. Antonio, the Mestizo, went in front. Then came

Gonzalo, the other Mexican. After him came the Chinaman, Sam Woe by name, who was the most elegant of our group, the only one with a whole shirt. He wore linen trousers, ankle-high heavy boots, dark cotton socks, and a fashionable straw hat. Sam carried two bundles, bulging and obviously heavy. He smiled constantly, was always in a good humor, and as we went on it became our most bitter grievance that no matter what we did or what bad luck we met with, nothing provoked him to anger. He told us that he had worked as a cook in an oil field but, so that we wouldn't get the idea he was carrying money on him, he lost no time in informing us that his earnings were deposited in a Chinese bank in San Luis Potosí.

Cotton-picking was not Sam's great passion (or mine), but it was a summer job and he thought he might as well add a few pesos to his capital, with which he hoped to open a small restaurant—Comida Corrida, 50 Centavos—in Tampico or thereabouts, in the autumn. He was practical. When we'd got well into the dense bush he cut himself a stick, hung one bundle over each end, balanced the stick across his shoulders, and trotted along in short rapid steps. He made the whole march in this maddening way, with no sign of fatigue and no variation in tempo, and expressed his astonishment that we stopped now and then for a short rest. We let fly at him, telling him that we were decent Christians while he was a low Chink hatched by a monstrous yellow dragon.

Next in line was the gigantic Negro, Charley, and he suited our company much better than the smart Chink, for Charley wore rags and had his bundle done up in old brown paper that, like ours, broke open on the march. Charley claimed to have come from Florida, but he couldn't convince me of it because he couldn't speak English fluently. His Spanish was also very limited, so I imagine that he either came from Brazil or had smuggled himself over from Africa. He obviously wanted to get to the States, and it would be easier for him as a Negro to get over the border, even if his English was not very good, than for a white man who spoke the language well. He was the only one who regarded cotton-picking as a welcome and profitable occupation.

Then there was Abraham, the little Negro from New Orleans, who wore a shirt as black as his skin, so that it wasn't easy to distinguish between the shreds of his shirt and the skin it tried to cover. Abraham was the only one who wore a cap, oddly enough a blue-striped cap of the kind worn by railroad stokers and engineers. He had no bundle, but he carried a coffee pot and a frying pan, and some food in a small canvas bag. Abraham was wily, cunning, cheeky, and ever in good spirits. He had a mouth organ on which he played that silly tune "Yes, we have no bananas" so often that on the second day we let loose on him with our fists.

Gonzalo said that Abraham stole like a crow, and Antonio said that he lied like a Dominican friar. On the third evening out, we caught Abraham stealing a slice of Antonio's dried beef, but we relieved him of it before he got it into his frying pan and solemnly explained to him that if we caught him stealing again we would deal with him according to the law of the bushland. We would try him, duly sentence him, then take a cord from one of our bundles and hang him on the nearest ebony tree, leaving a note pinned on his body to explain why he had been hanged. Whereupon Abraham told us that we would not dare to lay a finger on him, for he was an American citizen, "native-born," and would report us to the government in Washington if we so much as touched him. They would then come with a gunboat flying the stars and stripes and work vengeance on us. He was a free citizen "of the United States," could prove it with certificates, and so had the right to be tried before a proper court. When we told him that no gunboat flying the stars and stripes could sail into the bush, he said, "Well, Gentlemen, Sirs, just touch me with the tip of one finger and see what happens."

What happened was that we caught him a few days later stealing a can of condensed milk from the Chink. He brazenly claimed he'd bought the milk at a store in Tampico, but we gave him such a beating that he couldn't have held a pen to write to Washington. (Later, when he pilfered from others, that was, of course, none of our business.)

Then last in line there was Gerard Gales—that's my name. There's not much to say about me. In dress I was indistinguishable from the others, and I was going cotton-picking—laborious, underpaid work—because there was no other work to be had and I badly needed a shirt, a pair of shoes, and some trousers. Even so, they would have to come from a second-hand shop. Ten weeks' work at cotton-picking would never earn enough to buy them new.

The sun was already low when we began to look around for a place to pitch camp.

Before long we found a spot where high grass extended into the bush; we pulled out as much of it as was necessary to clear a camping ground and set fire to the surrounding grass, thereby gaining some freedom from insects and creeping vermin for the night. A freshly-burned grass area is supposed to be the best protection you can have if you are obliged to journey in these parts without the equipment of the tropical traveler.

We had a campfire, but no water to cook with. At this point the Chink produced a bottle of cold coffee. We had had no idea that he was carrying such precious stuff with him. He heated the coffee and obligingly offered us all a drink. But what was a bottle of coffee among six men who had been plodding along in the tropical sun for half a day without a drop of water? Furthermore, it was probable that we'd find as little water during the next day as we had found on this first afternoon. The bush is green, yes, the whole year through, but water is to be found only during the rainy season and then only in those spots where ponds and basins form.

So, no one who has not himself wandered the tropical bush can possibly realize the extent of the Chink's sacrifice. But none of us said "No, thank you." Everyone seemed to take it quite for granted that the coffee should be shared. And we'd have taken it equally for granted had the Chink drunk all his coffee himself. Half a day's march in waterless country isn't enough to make you turn robber for the sake of a cup of coffee, but three days in the bush may find you thinking seriously of murder for the sake of even a small rusty can of stinking fluid called water only because it is wet.

Antonio and I had some dry bread to munch. Gonzalo had some tortillas and four mangos. Charley had a few bananas. Abraham ate something furtively; I couldn't see what it was.

We made ready to sleep. The Chink put a piece of canvas on his sleeping place and then wrapped himself, head and all, in a large towel; Gonzalo rolled himself into his sarape; and I wrapped my head in a tattered rag as a protection against mosquitoes and promptly fell asleep. The others were talking and smoking around the fire and I've no idea when they turned in.

Before dawn, we were on our way. The trail through the bush was overgrown for long stretches. Saplings reached more than shoulder-high and the ground was so dense with cactus shrubs that they often covered the path. My bare calves were soon so scratched up that all sorts of insects were attracted to the blood.

Toward noon we arrived at a place where a barbed-wire fence ran along the right side of the trail and knew that we were near a farm. We kept the fence on our right, and after an hour or more arrived at a wide, open clearing overgrown with high grass. We searched the place and found a cistern—empty. A few rotten beams, some old cans, rusty corrugated iron sheets, and similar junk indicated an abandoned farm.

This was a disappointment, but we were not disheartened by it. In this part of the world farms are carved out of the bush, worked for ten or even twenty years, and then suddenly for one reason or another are abandoned. Within five years, often sooner, the bush has obliterated all signs of the men who once lived and worked there. The tropical bush devours more quickly than men can build. The bush has no memory; it knows only the living, growing present.

By four o'clock we got to another farm; an American family was living on it. I was well received, was given a good meal with the farmer, and was offered a place to sleep in the house. The others were fed on the patio and were allowed to sleep in a shed.

The farmer knew Mr. Shine, and told me that we had about another thirty miles to go. He said there was no water along the route and that the road was barely recognizable in some places, as it hadn't been used since that time three years ago. Mr. Shine now took his cotton to the Pozos station, on the other side of Ixtli. . . . "That place isn't quite so far from Shine's as the one you fellows are hiking from," he said. "The road's good too. At first there was no road to Pozos either, but since the oil men came they've made one. Now all the farmers around there use that station, and I'd advise you to take that road when you go back. By the way," he added, "I wonder why no one told you to go to Pozos in the first place?"

Why? Because to the men out recruiting pickers for the cotton farmers, what did it matter how we got to the job? "Ixtlixochicuauhtepec" they wrote out, and that ended their part in the matter. What concern was it of theirs to check out the route?

Because to the stationmaster it hadn't occurred that it might make a difference which station he made out the ticket for, or maybe he hadn't even known there was a choice, or, if he had, that the choice was between a three-day walk beating a path under a burning sun and a real road where we might even have been able to pick up a ride.

The next morning we were all given a generous breakfast, I once more eating at the family table. When we were getting ready to leave, the farmer rounded up enough bottles so that each of us could have a bottle of cold tea to take along, and we started out on those last thirty or so miles.

3

On the following day, about noon, we arrived at Mr. Shine's. He received us with real satisfaction, for he was short of hands.

Calling me into the house, he cross-examined me. "What?" he asked. "You want to pick cotton, too?"

"Yes, I must. I'm flat broke, You can see that, by my rags. And there's no work to be found in the towns. Every place is flooded with job-hunters from the States, where they're having their postwar slump. But when workers are needed here, they prefer to take on natives, because they pay them wages they'd never dare offer a white man, even if this Revolution is supposed to change all that."

"Have you picked before?" he interrupted me.

"Yes," I answered, "in the States."

"Ha, ha!" he laughed. "That's a different proposition. There, you can make a good thing of it."

"I did good enough."

"I believe it. They pay much better, and they can afford to pay, for they get better prices than we do. If we could sell our cotton to the States we could pay better wages, too. But the States won't let our cotton in; they want to keep the price up.

We have to depend on our home market, and that soon reaches the saturation point. Sometimes, when the States don't interfere, we can sell to Europe, but that's rare because they consider Europe their market.

"But now—what about you? I can't feed you or put you up in my house. But I need every hand that comes along, so I'll tell you what. I pay six centavos the kilo; suppose I pay you just two cents more than the others—otherwise you won't make as much as the niggers. Only don't tell this to the others, 'cause if they find out they'll give me lots of trouble. So that's how matters stand. I'm sorry."

"No reason for you to feel sorry," I said. "You pay me the same as the others. Don't let my white skin and blue eyes bother you. I understand how you feel. By all means, thank you."

"You and your friends can sleep over there in the old house. I built it and lived in it with my family until I could afford this new one here. Agreed? It's settled then."

The house to which the farmer referred was about five minutes' walk from his new place. It was the usual farmhouse of the region—poles and boards—and was built on piles so that the air moving under the floor kept the interior cool. It had only one room, and each wall had a door that also served as a window.

We entered the house by climbing the few rungs of a crude ladder set up against one of the doors. The room was completely empty. We found four old boxes lying about in the yard and brought them in to use as chairs. We would sleep on the bare floor.

Close to the house was a dried-up water hole. There was also a tank full of rain water that was several months old and teeming with tadpoles. I calculated there were about twenty-five gallons of water in the tank and we six men would have to make do with this for six or eight weeks. With three of us using the same water, we might be able to wash once a week.

Mr. Shine had already told us that we could expect no water from him; he was short of water, and had to provide for six horses and four mules. But, as he said, at this time of year it might possibly rain for two or even four hours every two weeks, and if we repaired the rain troughs we could collect quite a bit of water. Furthermore, there was a creek about three hours' walk away, where, if we chose, we could go to bathe.

On the slim chance that it might rain within the next two weeks, we all took a wash in an old gasoline can. We hadn't washed for three days.

I shaved. However down and out I may be, I always carry a razor, comb, and toothbrush. The Chink also shaved. Then Antonio came and asked if he could borrow my razor. He hadn't shaved for about two weeks, and looked like a pirate.

"No, my dear Antonio," I said, "shaving kit, comb, and toothbrush I lend to no one."

The Chink, encouraged by my refusal, said, smiling, that his poor razor would be blunted by such a strong beard, and there was no possibility of getting the razor sharpened here. He himself had only a fuzzy stubble. Antonio accepted these refusals without protest.

We got a campfire going in front of the house; the nearby bush supplied us with plenty of fuel. Then we sat around and cooked our suppers. I had rice and chile; a couple of the men fixed black beans and chile; someone else had beans and dried meat; while another fried some potatoes with a little bacon.

As we had to be ready for work at four o'clock the following morning, we prepared our corn bread for the next day. Then we tied up our miserable supplies and hung them from a crossbeam in the house, so that the ants and mice wouldn't relieve us of everything during the night.

A little after six, the sun went down. Within half an hour

the night was pitch black. Glowworms, with lights the size of hazelnuts, flew about us. We crept into our house to sleep.

The Chink was the only one who had a mosquito net. We others had to endure the most frightful torment from hordes of insects, and we cursed and raged as if that could have made any difference. I decided that I'd have to stand this agony for one night but that I'd take steps the next morning to do something about it.

Before sunrise we were up and about. Each of us swallowed what food we had at hand, and made off for the cotton field—an hour's walk. The farmer and his two sons were already there. They handed us an old sack apiece, which we slung from our necks. Tightening our belts around our ragged clothes, we started picking cotton, each to his own row.

Picking cotton is hard work, especially under a tropical sun. Sweat streamed from us, tiny flies crept into our ears, and mosquitoes stung us from every angle. It was an agony, and yet we kept on pulling cotton bolls from the plants, stuffing them into our sacks, while trying to breathe in the haze of cotton dust and fuzz that hung over each of our stooping bodies. No matter how hard we worked, we would earn little more than enough to buy food to keep alive. And that was what we wanted, just to keep alive; so we worked on.

If the cotton is well ripe and you've got the picker's knack, you can pick each bloom at one grasp. However, if the pods are not equally ripe it's necessary with more than half of them to give two or three good tugs to get the bloom off the plant and into the sack. With well-ripened cotton, and when the plants are well spaced, it's possible after some practice to pick with both hands; but with a middling crop and badly spaced plants, you may have to use both hands to pick one bloom. And another thing, you have to keep stooping all the time, for not all the blooms are at a convenient height; and at times, the cotton is close to the ground, where a heavy rainfall has flattened it, and it has to be pulled up.

Cotton is expensive stuff. Anyone who goes to buy a suit, a shirt, a towel, a pair of socks, or just a handkerchief soon discovers this. But the cotton-picker who does the toughest part of the work gets the smallest share of the cost of the finished product. For picking a kilo (about two pounds) of cotton we got six centavos. A kilo of cotton is a little mountain; to pick this much you've got to pluck out hundreds of pods.

We did this on a diet that could well be regarded as the very lowest on which man can remain alive. One day it was black beans and hot peppers, the next day rice (with tomatoes, if we were lucky), the following day, beans again, and then rice again. With it there was the bread we made that was either soggy or burned to a cinder; our months-old stinking rain water; and coffee made from beans that we roasted in frying pans, ground on a metate stone, and sweetened with the crude brown piloncillo sugar. The salt we used was sea salt, which we ourselves had to clean. A pound of onions a week we considered a positive delicacy; a strip of dried meat now and then was a sinful luxury that cut deep into our earnings. For we were determined to save our pennies in order to have rail fare to the next big town, where when the cotton-picking was over we hoped to find a new job.

Toward eleven o'clock, after nearly seven hours of continuous work, we were at the end of our strength. We rested in the shade of a few trees that were more than a ten-minute walk away and ate our dry pan-baked bread, which—mine anyway—was burned. Then we lay down to sleep for a couple of hours.

We woke with a ghastly thirst, and I went over to the farmer to ask for some water.

"I'm sorry, I haven't got any. I told you yesterday, didn't I, that I was short of water? Oh well, I'll let you have some today, but from tomorrow on bring your own water with you."

He sent one of his sons back to the house on a horse, and the young man soon came back with a can of rain water.

At four in the afternoon we stopped work so that we could get "home" to cook our food while there was still daylight.

That was when I moved out.

I had discovered a sort of shelter about two hundred yards away from the house. What purpose it served or might have served I had no idea. It had a palm-thatched roof but no walls. Because of this lack of walls the night breeze (when there was one) could freely circulate, keeping the place cool. In the center was a table, which I would use as my bed. The shelter lay higher than the house, had no shrubs close to it, and was a good distance away from the water tank and the dried-up water hole, so that I would be removed from the mosquito menace.

The giant Negro, Charley, wanted to share the shelter with me. He came over, looked around, and liked it. But suddenly he yelled out, "A snake! A snake!"

"Where?"

"There, right at your feet."

Sure enough, there was a snake twisting along the floor, a fiery red one, two feet or so long.

"It doesn't matter," I said. "That snake won't swallow me. The mosquitoes in the house up there are worse."

Charley disappeared.

After a while Gonzalo came over. The snake had gone in the meantime. Gonzalo liked the look of my new quarters and asked if I'd have any objection to his sleeping there also.

I said, "You may bunk here if you like. It's all the same to me."

He was staring at the floor. I looked too. It was a snake again, this time a beautiful green one.

"On second thought," he said, looking at the lively snake, "I'd better return to the house and sleep there. It's less noisy there, you see."

Snakes don't bother me. And in any case they'd hardly want to get up onto the table. And even if they did, it wasn't sure they'd bite me. And even if they did bite, they might not be poisonous. If all snakes were poisonous and all of them bit a sleeping man who had done them no harm, I would have been a goner long ago.

The following day twelve natives arrived to work with us. They came from a village in the bush, riding on mules, some without saddles or stirrups. Others had wooden saddles but no reins; instead of reins, the beasts had ropes looped around nose and jaw, for a kind of halter.

These men, of course, were more used to field labor in the tropics than we were because, with the exception of Gonzalo and Charley, all of us were townsfolk. But they picked cotton slower than we did, and on top of that they took a much longer siesta at noon. This, however, had nothing to do with us, and we hardly gave it a second thought.

Saturday was pay day, but we drew only enough to buy food for the coming week; to avoid carrying the germs of temptation in our pockets, we left the balance with Mr. Shine. On Sunday we knocked off at three so as to take our weekly bath, pull our sweaty clothes through the water, and send two of our gang to the nearest store for supplies—a four-hour trip. Sunday's work earned us about a kilo of bacon or five kilos of potatoes.

This time the Chink and Antonio had gone to buy the supplies. We had written down our various needs on corn husks. The hieroglyphics inscribed on these corn husks could be deciphered by the shoppers only because we'd verbally explained each fantastic symbol. It was dark when the Chink and Antonio returned from the store.

"What a miserable hike," grumbled Antonio.

"Oh, it wasn't so bad!" Sam tried to soothe it over.

"Shut up, you yellow son of a heathen," shouted Antonio. "How can you with your coolie past understand how I feel about packing goods like a burro?" He sank down onto a box which collapsed under his weight, and this further increased his rage.

"Listen, Antonio, why didn't you ask Mr. Shine for a mule or a burro?" I asked.

"But I did. He refused. He said to me and Sam: 'How can I lend you a mule or a burro? I know nothing about you, you've got no papers to identify you, and even if you did they would probably be fake. Besides, the papers wouldn't help me to buy a new burro if you ran off with it.' "

"Well, he's quite right, from his point of view," I said. "From our point of view, it's downright mean. But what can we do about it?"

Just as we were getting under way on the favored topic of workers the world over, expounding with more loquacity than wisdom the unjust conditions that divide men into exploiters and exploited, drones and disinherited, Abraham appeared with half a dozen hens and a rooster suspended on a cord, their feet tied up, their heads dangling. He dropped the birds before us, where they struggled to get on their feet and flap free of the cord that tied them.

"There you are, fellers, now you can get eggs off me." He grinned. "I'll let you have 'em cheap 'cause you're my workmates. Nine centavos each. Cost you ten and even twelve in town."

We stared first at the bundle of hens and then at the grinning Abraham. Not one of us had thought of going into the egg business like this, and yet it was so obvious, so simple, and required no special intelligence, so that any of us could have done the same. Sam the Chink showed no envy or jealousy, but only admiration for the enterprising Abraham, and perhaps some shame at having allowed himself to be beaten in setting up a sideline.

Thus in the course of one afternoon the disinherited and exploited worker Abraham became an owner, a capitalist. He had acquired productive hens while we had bought only food to be consumed. We had wondered why he had ordered no food from the store and had been prepared to deal with the pilfering of our supplies, which we had expected of him. Instead he was offering us future supplies of eggs in exchange for rice and beans or money. He was in business. At the worst, in case the hens went on strike, he could eat them, and the rooster too.

On the following day Abraham had four eggs for sale.

4

 We regarded eggs as a greater luxury than meat. And now that they were so temptingly close at hand and could be prepared more easily than any other food, so that we could get something better into us for breakfast than the usual thin coffee and piece of dry bread, we felt we would not and could not do without eggs. It suddenly seemed to us that without eggs we would fold up from undernourishment before the end of the harvest, or if we survived the harvest we'd be too feeble to go on to other work.

The slaves, said Abraham, who had it from his granddad, were generally kept in good condition, like horses. But no one worried about the condition of the "free" worker. If he got ill through malnutrition due to substandard living conditions because of low wages, he got sacked.

Opportunistic arguments of this kind were advanced by Abraham so as to ensure a ready and regular market for eggs. Such observations on man's condition were all the more acceptable to us since, generously enough, he supplied us with eggs on credit until the next pay day. Abraham did this purely out of the kindness of his heart because, as he explained it, he

27

did not want to see us, his dear fellow workers, fail from malnutrition in later life, that is, after the harvest.

Within three days we couldn't imagine how we had ever existed without eggs. We had eggs for breakfast, we took eggs along to the field for lunch, and of course we had eggs for supper. We were even baking eggs into our bread.

There was no doubt about it, Abraham understood chicken farming. Often he left the field as early as three to look after his hens. He gave them plenty of corn. Every other evening just at twilight he went off—he never said where—with a sack. He always returned with his sack full of corn long after we had turned in.

Those six hens and the rooster, apparently aware of our need, did their best to protect us from malnutrition, laying a generous supply of eggs in honest return for the abundant grain they received.

Well, the hens laid four eggs on the first day; on the second day, seven. On the third morning, lest we doubt his word, Abraham took us to the three old baskets he'd hung up for the laying hens and let us count the eggs for ourselves. There they were, seventeen eggs now. Having counted these eggs at sunrise, we doubted Abraham's word no more, not even when with beaming face one morning, as if he'd won in the national lottery, he informed us that the hens had laid twenty-eight eggs in one day! It was no concern of ours what Abraham did to his hens to get such results. The Chink said that the Chinese performed miracles in squeezing nutriment from a particle of earth or the last egg from a hen, but that Abraham outdid even them.

Abraham cut him short: "You're all a lot of fools. You know as little about scientific chicken farming as the farmers around here, who are the biggest fools of all. In Louisiana we know how to handle hens. I learned it from my grandmother, who gave me some good clouts before I got the hang of it, but now even the smartest farmer wouldn't stand a chance against me if I ran a chicken farm here. I'd show him how to make hens pay."

We just went on eating eggs. But the eggs took their revenge: they devoured us. They devoured our wages to the extent that none of us would reach his set target, whether it was for a new shirt, new trousers, or simply a railroad ticket to a place with better prospects. Even Sam, whose countrymen are often unjustly charged with preferring to run around naked rather than spend a penny on a necessity, owed Abraham a neat sum for eggs.

Compared to our first week we were living like princes now, thanks to the eggs, and also to a night rainstorm that provided us with enough rain water to wallow in baths.

Yet the rain lost us half a day's pay, turning the cotton field into a muddy swamp from which we could hardly lift our feet.

By the third pay day it was plain that we couldn't get along on the miserable wages paid us. At the end of the harvest we'd have barely two weeks' wages in hand, and all of that would be spent before we could march out of the bush and on to the next job, wherever it might be.

"It's those damned eggs!" said Antonio, as we sat around the fire talking things over. "Those eggs are enslaving us miserably."

"But we didn't have to buy them," I put in. "Abraham didn't force them onto us. He could have saved them up and sold them to the store."

"That'd be more work for him," said Gonzalo.

At this moment Abraham came back with his evening's corn and, overhearing us, threw his sack down. "So you're talking about eggs! Haven't I done right by you all? Every egg freshly laid! I'm entitled to my money, ain't I, fellers?"

"Nobody talked about not paying. If you don't know what we're talking about, better keep quiet," I told him.

"Listen," broke in Antonio, "we were saying that unless we give up the needless luxury of eggs we'll have worked all these weeks for nothing."

"Needless lux'ry, you call it?" Abraham yelled. "You want to walk aroun' like skel'tons when the cotton-pickin's over? Now I'm collectin' my money! Antonio, you owe . . . "

I didn't care who owed for how many eggs. I paid my own bill and left for the shelter to turn in. On the way I could hear squabbling over the accounts, although it must be admitted that Abraham seemed absolutely honest in his business relations with us. But as I was dozing off that night I resolved to do without eggs the next week.

At dawn on Monday, as I was making my way to the fire, I heard Antonio shouting: "Where are the eggs this morning, you black-as-coal Yank? I want five eggs!"

Abraham was counting the eggs in his baskets and continued as if he hadn't heard Antonio.

"Hey there, didn't you hear me? I want five eggs. Or shall I lay them myself?"

"What's this?" asked Abraham, all innocence. "I don't want to force my eggs on you and rob you of your hard-earned wages. You'd better save the money. You can get along without eggs, like you did the first few days here."

We rose up like one man against Abraham's new tune, against his interference with our established way of life.

"Who do you think you are, you black nobody, telling me what I should and should not eat," chimed in Gonzalo. "Give me six eggs at once or I'll smash your woolly skull in."

"All right," Abraham agreed, "if that's the way you want it I'll supply you with eggs, as before."

"Well, how else?" asked Sam Woe quietly. "Filst you tempt

us into eating eggs, and when we get used to them you tly to withhold. Give me thlee eggs!"

The Chink was right. Just when we'd got used to the eggs, their high food value, easy availability, and simple cooking, were we suddenly to be denied them because of Abraham's whim? Why should I deny my poor self, and torture my poor body with the sight of beautiful, fresh eggs sizzling merrily in the others' frying pans? "Give me six!" I ordered. And once I had eaten three fried eggs and boiled the others to take for lunch, my spirit was subdued and penitent.

So we kept on eating eggs.

One afternoon a few days later Mr. Shine stopped me on my way back from the field and talked about his farm, how he had started with sixty dollars of hard-earned money, how he had hacked the bush out with his own hands, and how he had widened a narrow, overgrown twelve-mile mule track into a road fit for his truck.

"It took me twenty years of hard, very hard work to build up this place. And yet we gringos, who helped make this part of the country what it is today, feel that we must be ready to get out on short notice and leave everything behind. These people—with some reason, I admit—hate us like poison because they fear for their political and economic freedom and independence, which means everything to them."

Mr. Shine wasn't the first North-American farmer to tell me this.

"Some years are very good. I've had as many as four crops of corn in the same year, something I'd never get back in the States. And I must say the cotton's very good this year, first-class fiber, if only I can get a decent offer for it. The trick is in knowing just how long to wait, just when to sell. But I can't understand what's happened to my hens. We've never had so few eggs as in these last weeks. My neighbors are also complaining about their hens, and they're wondering what's going on in their corn bins that they fill up in the evening and find a little lower in the morning. Same happens to me. Must be rats, I'd say."

That evening I told the gang what Mr. Shine had said about his hens.

"There you are, fellers, there's the true American farmer for you!" said Abraham. "They'd eat their own fingernails, they're so mean, and they begrudge the po'r hens a handful of grain—then complain that they're not layin'. How kin they if they're not rightly fed? Look at my hens! I don't spare the corn, so I get what I want from them. They only have to be well fed and properly treated, and then they do their duty. My good grandmother Susanne taught me that, and she was a clever woman, you can take it from me, fellers. And that's a fact! Another thing," he went on, "it's not the rats that get into the bins of those greedy farmers, it is the po'r starvin' hens which at night instead of sleeping prowl around to pick up a few kernels of corn lest they starve to death, po'r little animals."

And we listened to him. After all, Abraham had the proof of his chicken knowledge in eggs.

5

 That same evening we came unanimously to the conclusion that we had to eat properly to keep up our work power, but that at the same time we had to see to it that a certain sum was left over at the end of the harvest so that we shouldn't have worked for nothing, like slaves just for our keep—that therefore, in a nutshell, we weren't being paid enough. If we got eight instead of six centavos a kilo, we could just about scrape through.

With this thought in our minds we went to sleep.

The next morning as soon as the other workers arrived in the field, Antonio and Gonzalo went up to them and explained that we intended to ask for eight centavos a kilo from now on, plus two centavos a kilo retroactively. These people, natives and more independent than we were, especially since they all had their own parcels of land, readily agreed.

Then Antonio and Gonzalo and two of the other men went up to the scales and told Mr. Shine how matters stood.

"No," answered Mr. Shine, "I'm not going to pay that, and that's that! I'm not crazy! I've never paid that much. I don't make that much on the cotton."

"All right," said Antonio, "then we're packing up. We'll be off today."

One of the local men intervened: "Listen, señor, we'll wait another two hours. Think it over. If you say no, we'll saddle our mules. And we'll take good care that you don't get any more men."

With that the conference came to an end. The four returned to the field and reported Shine's answer. The men left the rows they were picking, went over to the trees, and lay down to sleep. While I was also making my way toward the trees, Mr. Shine called, "Hey, Gales! Come over here a moment!"

"Now," I said while approaching him, "if you think I'm going to act as a go-between you're quite mistaken, Mr. Shine. If I were a farmer I'd be on your side and I'd go with you through thick and thin. But I'm not a farmer. I'm a farm hand, and I stick with my fellow workers. You understand, don't you?"

"Yes, of course, Gales. In any case I'm not trying to win you over to my side. You couldn't get the cotton in alone. But let's have a quiet talk about it."

Mr. Shine lit a pipe. His elder son, who was about twenty-six, lit a cigar, and the other son, a fellow of twenty-two or so, peeled some filthy-looking paper from a piece of chewing gum and popped the gum into his mouth.

"You're the only white man among the pickers here, and as I'm already paying you eight you are really neutral and can talk with us. I take it you haven't told the other fellows that you're getting eight?" asked Mr. Shine, taking his pipe from his mouth.

"No," I said, "I haven't had the slightest reason for doing so."

The fact is I hadn't. But I knew that had the subject come up, not one of the men would have felt wronged at my taking that extra two centavos. It wasn't any skin off their backs. And not one even now would accuse me of not having brought the subject up. What good would it have done them to know? Some things we didn't find it necessary to talk about. Our common lot was something else again.

Dick, the older boy, climbed into the back of the truck, propped himself against a bale of cotton, and dangled his legs over the side. Pete, the younger one, seated himself at the steering wheel and dozed off, still chewing his gum.

The old man leaned against the truck and, swearing the while, fiddled with his pipe that now went out, now got choked, now needed refilling although the tobacco in it hadn't yet burned through. Only by the way he was handling his pipe did the farmer give any outward indication of the excitement that was fuming within him.

When about five minutes had passed without a word being spoken, Pete sat up and suddenly burst out: "You know what I'd do if I were in your shoes, Dad? I'd pay up and say no more about it."

"You'd pay up, would you?" Mr. Shine was furious. "The money doesn't come out of your pocket. That makes 'I'd pay up' very easy. All right then, I'll take it out of your money."

"You won't do any such thing, Dad! Or, if you do, you'll have to give me the money for the cotton sold. Otherwise it wouldn't be fair."

"Oh, don't make me laugh! The money for the cotton sold? Have I sold even a dime's worth yet? I tell you, Gales, no one's offered me a penny yet. And what prime cotton it is this year! It'd put the whitest snowflake in all Alaska to shame. And just look here"—he tore off a pod nearby and holding it close to my nose squeezed it between his fingers—"the softest down is like barbed wire compared with this. Well, Gales, say something! Don't stand there as if you'd lost your tongue!"

"But don't forget I'm neutral," I protested.

"All right, you're neutral. But you can still open your mouth."

All he wanted was someone with whom to argue.

Dick settled himself more comfortably in the truck and said slowly and deliberately, drawling out his words: "I'll tell you something, Dad——"

"You? You're the right one to tell me something!"

"All right then, I won't. I've got time. It isn't my cotton, you know, it's yours."

Dick withdrew into sulky silence. The old man flew into a rage. "Well, damn it all, speak up! Or must I stand here until the cotton rots?"

"You see, Dad, that's exactly what I mean: until the cotton rots. If the men leave, we won't get any more help from around here. And if we recruit men from the towns we'll have to pay more in fares than the whole thing's worth."

"Well, talk faster, can't you?"

"I must think what I'm going to say. Look here, Dad, it's rained once already. And it looks as if we're going to get a very early rainy season or maybe a whole week of strip rain. If we do, it'll be good-bye to the cotton for good. It'll all be beaten into the mud, and you'll have to look for someone who'll buy sand, let alone cotton. The quicker we get the cotton ginned and marketed, the better chance we'll have on the price. Once the market is saturated we'll be glad if we get rid of it at a loss of twenty or twenty-five centavos the bale; that is, if we can sell it at all. So far we've made very good time in picking, and should be among the first on the market."

"Damn it all, boy, you're damned well right! Four years ago I had to sell at thirty centavos below the starting price and stood there like a beggar bumming for a bit of bread. But I'm not so mad that I'll pay eight centavos! I used to pay only three, and when the cotton stood badly, four. No! I'd ten times rather leave it to.rot than give in!"

So saying he hit out at a shrub as though he wanted to raze the entire field with one swat. Then in his anger, another idea occurred to him.

"It's the foreigners who are to blame for this. They come here and incite our people. They can never get enough to stuff into their big mouths. Our people around here aren't dissatisfied. Yes, and you too, Gales, you're one of the agitators. You're one of those bolshies who want to turn everything upside down and take our land away from us, and even pull our beds out from under our backsides. But you got the wrong man in me. I've been in that racket too. I know my way about and I know how it's done. Only we didn't have any I.W.W. or any of that nonsense."

"As far as I'm concerned, Mr. Shine, you're quite at liberty to speak your mind. But, by the way, what makes you think I'm a Wobbly? I haven't given you any indications."

"I know your kind. You're trying to bring in your ideas here before this Revolution is over. It won't be long, though, before it'll have failed completely. Well, I didn't mean you exactly. But I won't pay eight and that's that!"

"Now listen, Dad"—Pete spoke without turning toward his father—"you're wrong about the foreigners, absolutely wrong. The four foreigners are picking more than the natives. The Indians only pick a bit because they see the foreigners at work, but they don't care about earning more. If they make one peso they're quite content. They prefer to have a five-hour siesta—that's much more important to them. You can bet your boots that without the foreigners we wouldn't be able to get the cotton in before Christmas."

"But I'm not paying, and that's the end of it."

"In that case I'll start the engine and we can drive home," Dick said dryly, and slowly came down from the truck.

The two hours agreed on were far from over, but the "locals" were getting restless. They caught their mules and began to saddle them. Just as some of them were about to mount, Antonio and Gonzalo jumped up, threw their wide-brimmed sombreros high into the air, and began to sing the song of the cotton-pickers, which I had taught them during our evenings around the campfire.

> "Cotton is worn by king and prince,
> Millionaire and president,
> But the lowly cotton-picker
> Sweats to earn each bloody cent. . . ."

The men immediately ceased handling their animals and stood as still as soldiers under orders. They had never heard the song before but with the instinct of the burdened they felt that this was their song, and that it was as closely allied to their strike, the first strike of their experience, as a hymn is allied to religion. They didn't know what the I.W.W. was, what a labor organization meant, what class distinctions were. But the singing they heard went straight to their hearts. The words were as the breath of life to them, and the song welded them together as into a block of steel. A first dim awareness of the immense power and strength of the working people united in a common purpose was awakened in them.

By the time the first refrain was repeated, the whole field was singing. I knew what was likely to happen if the last refrain were reached without the desired answer having been received. I knew it from experience.

The song, so simple and monotonous in its melody, but in its resounding rhythm as springy as fine steel, infected me. I couldn't help it. I began to hum it too.

"Of course, you would!" said Mr. Shine, half sarcastically, half matter-of-factly. "I knew it!"

At the second refrain the men, who had been standing around near their mules in a loosely formed group, turned toward Mr. Shine; they stood as one man, their song taking on a provocative, direct significance.

Mr. Shine fumbled nervously at his belt to unfasten his revolver holster, only to fasten it again with a look of embarrassment, in which could be detected also shame, and even resignation.

"Confound it all!" he exclaimed. "They look as if they mean business."

"So they do," Pete said, still chewing. "And once they've gone, we'll have the devil's own job to get them to come back again."

"Right," said Mr. Shine. "I'll pay eight, but only from today. What's paid is paid and there's going to be no back pay. Gales," he turned to me, "would you be good enough to call the men?"

I ran over and called them together.

"Well, what about it?" the men asked Mr. Shine as they approached the scales.

"It's all right, it's settled," he said, half irate and half condescending. "I pay eight per kilo, but——"

Antonio didn't let him finish: "And what about the kilos we've already picked?"

"I'll pay the difference of two centavos. But now get to work so we can get the cotton in before the rains come."

"Hurrah fo' Mister Shine!" shouted Abraham.

"Keep your mouth shut, damn you. Nobody's asked you to shout!" roared the farmer in a fury.

"But what am I going to do with you, Gales?" he asked, keeping me back as the men were leaving. "You're already getting eight."

"Yes," I said, "so that evens things up."

"No. One man's pay won't make much difference to me. After all, you're the only white in the gang. I'll give you ten."

"With back pay?" I laughed.

"With back pay. I'm a fair businessman. Now, why are you hanging around? Hurry up, get along with the work. We've wasted, God knows, practically an hour talking. And any hour the rain might come.

Then, turning to his two sons, who were just in the act of hanging up the scales, he said: "I'm going to make you pay, you two; take my word for it!"

6

Nothing much happened during the following three weeks. One day was like the next—picking cotton, cooking, eating, sleeping, picking cotton . . .

Then one afternoon, when I got back from the cotton field, I went over to the big house to see if Mrs. Shine could sell me some bacon, or loan it to me until Sunday, as I'd forgotten to ask the fellows to get me some when they went shopping.

"Certainly, Gales, you can have it for cash or on loan, just as you like."

"All right. I'll buy it. The boss can charge it to me on pay day."

As she was weighing the bacon, Mr. Shine returned from town with the mail and a few purchases.

"You've come just at the right moment, Gales," he said. "I've got some news for you."

"For me? Where from?"

"Direct from town. While I was at the store I met Mr. Beales, the crew manager from Oil Camp 97, an acquaintance of mine. He was sitting there drinking one bottle of beer after another, with a grim face. He's in a fix. They've had some trouble at the derrick. It seems they were changing the drills—

eights for tens—when one of the pipes kicked out and injured a driller's right arm. One of the native laborers had been careless—nothing new, the same kind of thing has happened before —and didn't secure the pipe in time. The driller's an experienced man, a reliable fellow, and they don't want to lose him. So they're looking for a good temporary man to take his place until he can come back. It'll be three or four weeks before he's fit for work again. It's a ticklish time for them just now. They're drilled to seven hundred feet and are on clay, so if they don't get a good driller they might get a bend in the bore pipe. You've worked in the oil fields and know what this would mean—expense and a loss of time. The drillers and tool dressers would have to be laid off—maybe the whole camp."

"You're telling me," I replied. "But it's the sort of thing that can happen in the best-managed field, no matter how careful the men are."

"Could be. I don't understand anything about drilling," Mr. Shine said, anxious to go on. "Now the manager's wondering what to do next. He's already worked one shift himself, but he can't carry on like that. If he telegraphs his company in the States it'll take another three to four days before he gets a new man here, and then it's not certain that he'll get a good relief man. You know a good man normally won't take on a job for three weeks and maybe risk missing out on a good, six-month job. So I said to the manager, 'Mr. Beales, I've got just the man you're looking for.' "

"But I still don't see where I come in," I said. "Why do you do this for me? Are you trying to get rid of me?"

"Now, wait a minute, Gales. I'm on the level with you. In three, or at most four days we'll have the cotton picked. What are you going to do then?"

"I don't know yet. I'll wait and see. I may go north or south, or I may go east or west. Actually I was thinking of tramping down to Guatemala, Costa Rica, and Panama—maybe to Colombia. I've heard there's a good deal of oil being pumped down there."

"Fine!" said Mr. Shine. "That's just what I thought. It's all the same to you where you go. There'll be time enough, later on, to visit Guatemala and all the other beauty spots waiting just for you. So I said to the manager: 'Well, I've got a fellow at the farm, helping me with my cotton crop, a white man, honest all through, a very reliable fellow, with experience in drilling, tool dressing, and all that goes with it.' I had to lay it on a bit thick, you know, Gales, to get results. 'Well, Mr. Beales,' I said, 'I'm going to send the man down to you!' Now what do you say, old chap, eh?" Mr. Shine asked me, grinning all over his face. "So down you go to the store tomorrow morning. The storekeeper knows the way to the camp; he'll direct you. You'll be at the camp in time to sit right down to a full-sized meal."

The part about the meal was tempting.

"If you find you can't manage the job, you won't have lost much. Whatever happens, you'll get a day's pay and on top of that you'll have some good eats, for one day," Mr. Shine added.

I really didn't have to waste much thought on the offer. There was only three or four days' work left here, hard and ill-paid work. At the oil field you also had to work a twelve-hour day as there were only two shifts, but at least you were not working in that blistering sun. Moreover, you got ice water to drink, and as much of it as you wanted. But above all you got, as Mr. Shine had rightly said, decent food, with plate, knife, fork, spoon, cup, and glass on a table that might have been crudely knocked together but was a table all the same, and there was a real bench on which to sit. Black beans, hard as pebbles, would cease to be a major part of every meal. And they didn't sleep without bedding on the bare floor, but in clean camp beds with soft mattresses and well protected by thin veils of mosquito netting. There would be a toilet. You could shower every day. I had quite forgotten that there were such things in the world. These workers lived in good houses, and had a hospital and all conveniences in their camps.

So I thanked Mrs. Shine but changed my mind about the bacon. When I got back to the campfire the most important thing as far as I was concerned was to settle my egg account with Abraham. If I'd remained even ten centavos in his debt he'd have pursued me in my dreams right down to Cape Horn.

I arrived at the oil camp and reported to the manager. He was an American. All the managers, high employees, and even specialized workers in the oil fields were mostly foreigners, as practically all the companies exploiting the oil in this country were either American, English, or Dutch and they preferred to give employment to their own compatriots. Mr. Beales didn't look a bit surprised to see his new driller in such rags and tatters as no man in his own country would ever have dared walk around in. He obviously didn't care what I wore; he needed a reliable driller.

The workers at the camp were glad that Dick, the sick driller, had a substitute and would be coming back. He was a likable guy who had worked in the camp ever since the first planks went up. They fixed me up, one man bringing me a shirt, another pants, another socks, another working gloves and shoes.

When I'd finished my first shift, Mr. Beales said: "You can stay on until Dick comes back, at full driller's pay."

This certainly was very good news. But Dick recovered faster than anybody had expected, so at the end of a week's work I had to be on my way again. When I left, Dick gave me twenty dollars extra out of his own pocket, for travelling expenses, and, as he said, to treat myself to something good.

When the manager paid me off he said, "Listen, Gales, couldn't you hang around in the vicinity for another week or so?"

"Yes," I replied. "Easily. I could go to Mr. Shine's and stay there for a while. Why?"

"There's a fellow in one of the fields here who wants to take a two-week vacation to go up to the States to see his folks. You could fill in as his substitute—beginning of the month."

"Agreed," said I. "You can leave a message at the store for me, care of Mr. Shine, when you need me."

"Right, that's settled!" said Mr. Beales.

So I went back to Mr. Shine's the next day and asked him if I could put up for a while in the shelter.

"Certainly, Gales," he said. "Stay as long as you like."

I told him about my oil field chance, and then asked about the other pickers, my former companions.

"Oh, them. Well, the tall nigger went the day after you—up to Florida, I think. The short one, the one called Abraham, turned out to be a scoundrel——"

"How do you mean?"

"Well, he sold me some hens—good layers, he swore—that he'd bought from some peasants, I found out later, for one peso apiece. Sold them to me for two and a half pesos each. The hens were well fed, heavy, good to look at, so I paid the price. But that black devil, he got me on the part about layers. They're not laying one egg among them. Oh, well—I s'pose they're worth the price for meat."

"And what about the Chink and the two Mexicans?"

"They walked by here—early—on Monday. I saw them from the window. As far as I know, they went to the Pozos

station. By the way, why do you want to live in that shelter?
You could stay in the house."

I laughed. "No, Mr. Shine, I had enough of that house. I
wouldn't stick the tip of my boot inside it. It's a real mosquito
hell."

"Well, suit yourself. I lived in it with my family for ten
years and we weren't troubled by mosquitoes. But you may be
right. If a house like that hasn't been used for some time, and
isn't properly aired, all sorts of vermin gather. Now and again
I have the horses and mules driven up that way because of the
good grass and the water hole. But I haven't been up there for
months and I've no idea what the place is like now. Anyhow, it
doesn't matter to me where you set up house. You're no worry
to me."

So once again I rigged myself up in my shelter. This time I
made my fire right in front of it. There was no point in
making it near the little house where we'd had our campfire
discussions; no one was there to talk with now.

7

    I lived in wonderful solitude, my sole companions
the lizards. After I'd been there about three days,
two lizards got so used to me they forgot their innate timidity
and went after the flies that hovered around my feet in search
of crumbs.

I spent my days puttering around in the near bush, observing animals and their behavior; and the animals of the bush
came and went through my open shelter, as was their right. I
had brought back some old magazines from the oil camp and
now had time for reading.

I could wallow in water. There had been several good
downpours and the water tank was a third full, for we'd
mended the rain troughs, of course. I could wash; I could even
afford the luxury of washing twice a day.

Now I was able to buy what I wanted in the store; I had
plenty of money and I treated myself well. I was neither
thirsty nor hungry. I hadn't a care in the world. I was a free
man in the free bush, taking my nap when I pleased, roaming
about when and where and as long as I liked. It was a good life
and I enjoyed it to the full.

I drew the water I needed from the tank that lay by the old

house. It had been lively there while my companions lived in the house; there were arguments around the campfire, words over a pinch of salt that one had taken without asking the owner, endless wrangles about whose turn it was to bring firewood, and the like. As I thought back on those vivid scenes, the house seemed eerily lonely and still. Every time I went over there to get water I had the urge to look inside to see if anyone had left anything behind. But then again, I liked the spooky silence that brooded over the place, and I hesitated to disturb it. It fitted in with the solitariness of the surrounding bush, as well as with the seclusion of my own life. So I suppressed the desire to go up the ladder and peep in. Of course I knew that the house would be empty, absolutely empty. No one would have left anything behind, not even the rags of an old shirt; for, to fellows like us, everything has its value. I even began to grow used to the air of mystery that hung over the place. I liked to think that perhaps the ghost of an old Aztec priest, unable to rest, had now fled from the bush into the house to find some repose from his restless wanderings.

One day when I went to get water, I noticed a blue-black spider with a shiny green head hunting her prey along a wall of the house. She'd run like lightning for a few inches, stop, lie in wait awhile, and then run again a short distance and wait again. Zigzagging in this way, she completely covered three feet on one plank of the wall. Not a single spot had been left uncrossed. Here and there she left a fine thread behind her, not to trap and ensnare any insects that might climb up the plank, but to slow their progress so that after searching and returning from neighboring planks she could spring at her prey and take it in one leap. This spider takes her prey in leaps. She springs at the insect from behind and seizes it by the neck so that whatever weapons of self-defense it may have, whether they are spikes, claws, or jaws, it has no chance to use them.

I'd been observing this type of spider for days and weeks on end during my frequent spells out of work, and this one immediately attracted my attention. I wanted to test her field of vision and discover what she'd do if she herself were attacked and pursued. I put my can of water on the ground and forgot that I'd been intending to cook myself some rice.

I moved my hand to and fro a fair distance above the spider. She reacted immediately. She became uneasy and her zigzag runs began to get irregular as she tried to escape from the great Something that might have been a bird. But the smooth plank offered no hiding place. She waited a while, ducked slowly and carefully, and then suddenly and quite unexpectedly leaped half an arm's length to another board on the wall. The leap was as sure as if it had been executed on the level. The other board had a crack in it, so that it offered some refuge.

However, I allowed the spider no time to find the best spot. I took a thin twig and touched her lightly, forcing her to choose another route. She rushed away at frantic speed, but wherever she fled she always ran into the offensive twig which touched her head or her back. So she ran in all directions, always pursued by the twig which gave her no chance to get set for a leap. Suddenly, however, just as I was twigging her on the back, she turned around and, in a frantic rage and with impressive courage, attacked the twig. To a creature of her size—she was about an inch and a half long—the twig must have seemed an object of massive proportions and supernatural powers. Every time I withdrew the twig, which evidently made her think she had beaten back or at any rate intimidated her enemy, she tried to reach the protecting crack. Finally she did defeat me and found refuge there, but it wasn't enough to hide her completely; half of her was still exposed.

I now slapped my hand flat against the wall. The spider promptly reappeared and hurried off, higher up, where she found a more favorable cavity in which she was now almost completely concealed.

To chase her out of there too, and see what she'd do in the last extremity, I slapped the wall with such force that the whole house shook.

The spider didn't re-emerge. I waited a few seconds. When I was just about to hit the wall another time, something inside the house fell over with a thump.

Whatever could it be? I knew the inside of the house. There was nothing, absolutely nothing in there that could fall with such a strange sound. It could only have been a board or a chunk of wood; and yet, to judge from the noise, it was neither of these. It sounded more like a sackful of maize. But when I recalled the noise, I realized there had been something strangely hard about it too. So it couldn't have been a sackful of maize.

It would have been simple enough to climb the few rungs of the ladder, push open the door, and look inside. But some inexplicable feeling held me back. It was as if I were afraid I'd discover something unspeakably horrible.

I picked up my can of water and went back to my shelter. I persuaded myself that it wasn't a fear of seeing something horrible that was stopping me from going into the house. I said to myself: "You have no business in the house; you have no right to go in there, and in any case whatever is in there is no concern of yours." That's how I excused myself.

But when I was sitting by my fire, wondering what thing it could have been, a strange idea came to me: Someone had hanged himself in the house, some time ago; the rope had rotted or the neck had putrefied, and my striking at the wall had shaken the body, so that the corpse had fallen. It had sounded as if a human body had toppled over and the head had struck the floor.

But of course this idea was ridiculous. It only showed where your imagination could lead you if you shied away from looking at the facts. When you're in this state of mind, a tree trunk in the field could be a bandit waiting in ambush. Besides, in the tropics nobody would hang himself. In this part of the world suicide is rare; no day is gray enough for it. And if someone really did want to do it, why, he'd go into the bush where within three days the only part of him that would still be recognizable would be the buckle of his belt.

Whenever I went to get water I made a point of not looking into the house; I even avoided looking for any chink through which I could peep. The vague, the mysterious meant more to me than a possibly prosaic explanation. But when I sat by the fire in the evening or lay awake at night, my thoughts would turn to what might be inside the house.

On Saturday I went to Mr. Shine and asked if there'd been any message from the oil camp. But Mr. Shine hadn't gone to the store all week, and wouldn't be going the following week either. As Monday was the first of the month and the driller whose place I was to take could be starting his vacation then, I decided to go down to the store myself on Sunday morning. I would take my bundle with me and be ready to start off at once if word had come through. That way I could be in the camp on Sunday afternoon. If there was no message I'd know that the driller was either not going on vacation or that he'd made some other arrangement. In that case I'd continue on to the station and simply carry out my plan of going to Guatemala.

Early Sunday morning I went to get water for my coffee. I'd got the water and was already past the house when I decided that, after all, I'd go inside and see what there was to see. If I didn't, the thought of it would probably plague me for months to come.

I climbed the few rungs of the ladder and pushed open the door. Something was lying by the wall to my right—a large bundle. I couldn't see what it was right away, in the dawn light.

I stepped over to it. It was a man. Dead!

It was Gonzalo.

Gonzalo, dead.

Murdered!

His ragged shirt was black with dried blood. A ball of cotton, crumpled in his right hand, was likewise caked with blood. He had a stab in the back, and further stabs in the chest, the right shoulder, and the left arm.

Obviously the body had been propped up against the wall; when I had struck, it had fallen sideways and the head had hit the floor.

I searched his pockets—five pesos and eighty-five centavos. He should have had at least twenty-five to thirty pesos.

So it had been for the money.

A little canvas tobacco pouch lay open beside him. There were a few corn husks on the floor. He had been attacked while rolling himself a cigarette right there where he now lay.

The Chink and Antonio had been the last to leave the house. The Chink wasn't the murderer. He wouldn't so much as touch anyone for the sake of twenty pesos; he was far too clever for that. Those twenty pesos would have cost too dear for the Chink.

Antonio then.

I'd never have thought it of him.

I put the money back into Gonzalo's pocket and left him where he lay.

Then I wedged the door into position as I'd found it and left the house.

I gave up the idea of making coffee and set off at once. I went to Mr. Shine and told him that I was going to the store, and that if there was nothing doing at the oil camp I'd continue on my way.

"Didn't you feel lonely in your airy apartment, Gales?" he asked.

"No," I said. "There was so much to see and so many things to watch that the time passed very quickly."

"I thought you might have moved into the house. After all, it is a house."

"I told you when I came back from the oil field that it was swarming with mosquitoes."

"My two nephews are coming on a visit at New Year's. It'll be a holiday for them. I'll put them in there, and they can do as they like. They can make a start by smoking out the mosquitoes. Well, Gales, good luck to you!"

We shook hands and off I went.

Why should I have said anything? No one would think that I was the murderer, for hadn't I left before all the other fellows and been working at the oil camp all the time? If I had said something about it, there would have been endless questions and comings and goings and who knows what else, and I should never have been able to get to the oil field in time.

8

I was paid off when the driller returned from his vacation. One of the trucks took me to the station and from there I traveled on to a small town on the coast. I didn't stop long but went straight on to the next sizable town so that, provided I didn't change my plans again, I could get to Guatemala within a few days.

While I was in town I wanted to keep my ear to the ground and find out how things were in the south, whether there was anything behind the rumors of new oil fields, what the chances of employment were or whether I wouldn't do better to make tracks for the Argentine. But I heard too much about the mass unemployment down there. Ghastly stories I heard. Eighty thousand in the gutter in Buenos Aires alone, just looking for a chance to get out of there. Anyhow, it couldn't be worse than it was in Mexico.

I went over to the park and sat around on a bench. I had a shoe shine, drank a glass of ice water, and, feeling at peace with myself and all the world, was just about to take a siesta when I noticed that an acquaintance was sitting on a bench opposite me.

I went over to him. "Hello, Antonio," I said. "How are you? What are you doing here?"

We shook hands. He was very pleased to see me. I sat down beside him and told him that I was looking for a job.

"That's fine. I've been working in a bakery here for two weeks, baking bread and cakes. You could start in right away; they're looking for an assistant. You ever worked as a baker?"

"No. I've had a hundred different jobs, I've even been a camel drover—and what a goddamned job that is—but I've never been a baker."

"Fine!" said Antonio. "In that case you'll be all right. If you really were a baker or knew anything about baking, it'd be no good. The owner's a Frenchman; he knows nothing about baking. If you tell him that pepper'll improve the loaf, he'll believe you. Of course he'll ask you if you're a baker and you must tell him without batting an eyelash that you've been in the trade ever since you were a boy. The master baker is a Dane, a ship's cook who jumped ship. He knows nothing about baking, either. His worry is that some day someone who really knows something about baking will get a job there. That would be the end of the Dane and his master-baking. Yes, a real baker would size him up in less than ten minutes. So if the master asks you anything, you say the very opposite of what you say to the owner. Get the idea? You must tell the master baker that it's the first time in all your life you've seen the inside of a bakery. Then he'll take you on at once and be quite chummy with you."

"I can play that game," I said. "What's the pay?"

"One twenty-five a day."

"Bare?"

"Don't make me laugh. With room and board. Soap is free, too. By all means it's better than cotton-picking, I can tell you."

"What's the food like? Any good?"

"Well, it's not too bad."

"Mmmmm . . . "

"But you always get enough."

"I know the stomach fillers only too well."

Antonio laughed and nodded. He rolled himself a cigarette, offered me one which I didn't take, and after a few puffs, he said: "Between ourselves, the food's all right. The bakers and pastry cooks use eggs and sugar; it's a real pleasure to handle the food. Understand, a dozen eggs here or there aren't missed, and three eggs quickly broken into an odd cup and beaten up with some sugar helps the diet along. If you do this three or four times during the night, you feel fine."

"What are the hours then?"

"They vary. Sometimes we start at ten at night and work until one, two, or three in the afternoon—sometimes until five."

"That makes fifteen to nineteen hours a day then?"

"About that, but not always. Sometimes, generally on Tuesdays and Thursdays, we don't start until twelve."

"It's not exactly tempting," I said.

"But we might as well work there until we can find something better."

"Of course," I said. "If there were thirty-six hours in the day there'd be plenty of time to look around for something better. Ah well, I'll give it a try."

The thought that from now on I would be working with a murderer day and night, eating from the same pot, perhaps sleeping in the same room, this thought didn't occur to me at once. Either I'd sunk so low morally that I'd lost all feeling for such niceties of civilization, or I'd moved so far ahead of my time and so far above the moral standards of the day that I understood every human action, and neither took upon myself the right to condemn nor indulged in the cheap sentimentality of pity. For pity is also a condemnation, even if not so recognized, even if it is unconscious. Should I have felt a horror of Antonio, a revulsion against shaking his hand? There are so many thieves and murderers on the loose with diamonds on their fingers and big pearls in their neckties or gold stars on their epaulettes, and decent people think nothing of shaking hands with them, but even regard it an honor to do so. Every class has its thieves and murderers. Those of my class are hanged; others are invited to the president's ball and complain about the crimes and immorality of workmen like me.

When you have to struggle hard to get a crust of bread, you find yourself down in the mire, floundering among the scum of humanity.

I felt the blood rushing to my head as these thoughts went round in my mind. Antonio suddenly brought me back to earth with the question: "Do you know who else is in town?"

"How should I know? I just got here last evening."

"Sam Woe, the Chink."

"What's he doing here in Tampico?"

"You know he was always talking about the eating house he was going to open——"

"You mean he opened one?"

"You bet he did. When a Chink like Sam Woe makes up his mind to do something, he does it. He runs his business with a fellow countryman."

"You know, Antonio, you and I haven't the flair for such things. I'm quite sure that if I were to open a restaurant, people would start being born without stomachs, just to make sure I didn't get a break."

Antonio laughed. "That's my luck too. I've had a cigarette stall, a confectionary booth; I've lugged ice water around, and tried God knows what else. I hardly ever sold anything, and I went broke every time."

"I think, Antonio, it's because we can't bring ourselves to downright swindling. And you have to know how to swindle if you want to be a success in business."

"I suppose we should go and look up the Chink. He'd be pleased to see you too. I like to eat out now and then, for a change, you know. You can get sick of the same old grub where you work."

So, we went off to the Yellow Quarter where the Chinese lived and had their shops and restaurants. Very few of them had businesses in other parts of the town. They liked to crowd together.

Sam was genuinely pleased to see me. He kept pressing my hand, laughing and prattling. He invited us to sit down, and we ordered a comida corrida.

Chinese eating houses are all much alike in this country. They have simple, square wooden tables, frequently not more than three of them, with three or four chairs to each. In view of the number of dishes you get, not more than three very good-natured customers can sit at one table at the same time. You can usually see what's going on in the kitchen from where you sit. The nature and number of dishes is the same in all the Chinese places in town. That's how they rule out unfair competition among themselves.

Sam had five tables. On each table stood a big-bellied, reddish-brown clay water jug of an ancient Aztec pattern. Then there was a glass bottle containing oil and another one with vinegar. In addition, there were a big bowl of sugar and several small bowls, one with salt, one with a reddish powdered pepper, and one with chile sauce. Half a teaspoon of the hot chile sauce in your soup is enough to make it absolutely unfit to eat.

Sam served the customers while his partner, with the help of a Mexican girl, looked after the cooking. First we were given a chunk of ice in a glass which we filled with water. Next, we got a large roll, there called a bolillo, and the soup followed. It's always one variety of noodle soup or another. Antonio scattered a large soupspoonful of green chile sauce into his soup, and I took two heaping ones. I've already said that half a teaspoon of this fiery sauce seasons the soup so highly that it's impossible for a normal person to eat. But then, I'm not normal. While we were still dipping into our soup, the meat arrived, with fried potatoes, a dish of rice, a dish of beans. Now came a dish of stew. All the courses were put on the table at the same time.

Then, as usual, the swapping began. Antonio swapped his beans for tomato salad, which he prepared himself at the table, and I swapped my stew for an omelette.

Now Antonio put his rice into his soup; if he'd kept his beans he'd have put them in as well. Apparently he got enough beans at the bakery, but tomato salad was a treat.

I shook a layer of pepper onto my meat and another layer onto the fried potatoes. Then I seasoned the rice with chile sauce and sweetened the beans with sugar.

At the end of the meal we were each served a dulce—a sweet—and I had café con leche, that is, coffee with hot milk, but Antonio took only the hot milk.

Antonio and I exchanged small talk while eating. We didn't want to spoil our digestion by taxing our brains with profundities.

For our meal we paid fifty centavos each, all included. It was the usual price in a Chinese restaurant, a café de chinos.

And now we sailed along to the bakery. I went into the pastry shop and asked a clerk if I could see the boss.

"Are you a baker?" the owner asked me.

"Yes, baker and pastry cook."

"Where were you working last?"

"In Monterrey."

"Good. You can start tonight. Free room, board, laundry,

and I pay you one peso twenty-five a day. Wait a moment," he added suddenly. "Are you good on cakes, cakes with fancy icing?"

"In my last job in Monterrey I did nothing but cakes with fancy icing."

"Fine. But I'd better have a word with my master baker and hear what he says. He's a first-class man. You can learn a lot from him."

He took me into a dormitory, where the master was in the act of putting on his shoes, getting ready to go out.

"Here's a baker from Monterrey who's looking for work. See if he's any use to you." The boss went back to his office and left the two of us alone.

The master, a short, fat fellow with freckles, didn't hurry himself. He finished putting on his shoes and then seated himself on the edge of his bed and lit a cigar. When he'd taken a few puffs he looked at me suspiciously, looked me up and down and said: "Are you a baker?"

"No," I said. "To tell you the truth, I don't know much about baking."

"Really?" he said, still suspicious. "Do you know anything about cakes?"

"I've eaten them," I said, "but I've no idea how they're made. That's just what I want to learn."

"Well, have a cigar. You can start tonight at ten sharp. Would you like something to eat?"

"Not just now, thank you just the same."

"All right. I'll have a word with the old man. Now I'll show you your bed." It seemed he'd lost all his mistrust of me, and was very friendly.

"I'll make a good baker and pastry cook out of you if you pay attention to what I have to tell you and don't try bringing in new-fangled ideas of your own. That would never do you any good around here."

"I'll be most grateful to you, señor. I've always wanted to become a baker and pastry cook of the first order."

"You can have a nap now if you want one, or you can have a look around the town—just as you like."

"All right," I said, "I'll take a walk in the town."

"Well, ten o'clock, don't forget."

9

  I met Antonio, as agreed, in the park.

"Well?" he greeted me from the bench where he sat.

"I'm starting tonight."

"That's fine. Maybe later on I might hike down to Colombia with you."

I sat down beside him.

I couldn't think of anything to talk about and, searching in my mind for some subject of conversation, it occurred to me that this might be a good moment to mention Gonzalo. Actually I wasn't so much interested in talking about it as in observing his reaction and seeing how a man with murder on his conscience would behave when someone surprised him by disclosing that he knew all about the crime.

There was, no doubt, a certain risk involved. If Antonio discovered I knew he was a murderer, he'd make it his business to do away with me at the first chance. But I was prepared to run the risk; the very danger made me itch to throw my card on the table face up. I wouldn't be taken by surprise and was quite able to defend myself, although I would certainly avoid tramping through the bush, or going to Colombia, with him as my only companion.

"Do you know, Antonio," I said suddenly, out of nowhere, "that you're wanted by the police?"

"Me?" He seemed quite astonished.

"Yes, you!"

"What for? I don't know of anything I've done wrong."

It sounded very genuine, a bit too genuine to be on the level, I thought.

"For murder! Murder and robbery!"

"You're nuts, Gales. Me wanted for murder? You're badly mistaken. True, I was mixed up with Emiliano Zapata, but no murder. It must be someone else with the same name."

"Not a matter of mistaken identity," I said, getting tired of that cat and mouse play. I let loose, almost shouting: "Did you know that Gonzalo is dead?"

"What?" he shouted, even louder than I had.

"Yes," I said, very quietly now, yet watching him intently, "Gonzalo is dead; murdered and robbed."

"Poor devil. He was certainly a good guy," Antonio said sympathetically.

"Yes," I agreed, "he was a decent fellow. It's a pity. Where did you see him last, Antonio?"

"In the house, where we all had been sleeping during the harvest."

"Mr. Shine told me that the three of you—you, Gonzalo, and Sam—left his place together."

"If Mr. Shine says that, he's mistaken. Gonzalo stayed behind. Only the two of us, Sam and I, went to the station to catch the train."

"I don't understand," I put in. "Mr. Shine was standing at the window and definitely saw the three of you."

At this, Antonio gave a short laugh and said: "Mr. Shine is right, and I'm right too. The third man with us wasn't

Gonzalo but a man from nearby, a native who came to buy the hens from Abraham because he thought he'd get them cheap. But Abraham left two days before and had already sold them, to Mr. Shine I think."

"In the house where you last saw Gonzalo," I said, slowly now, "I found him murdered and robbed. That is to say, he hadn't been robbed of everything; the murderer had left him a little over five pesos."

"I wish I could be serious about this tragic story," said Antonio, smiling slightly to himself, "but I can't help laughing. The rest of Gonzalo's money is in my pocket."

"There you are! That's just what I've been talking about."

"You may have been talking about it your way, Gales," replied Antonio, "but I won the money from him. Sam knows all about it; he was there at the time. Sam lost five pesos himself. He would have a stake in it."

This was a strange story indeed.

"Sam, myself, and the Indian neighbor, we left the house together. Gonzalo wanted to stay behind and have a good sleep. I went with Sam by train to Celaya. Sam went on by train, and I did the rest of the way here partly on foot and by riding freights for a few stretches."

What Antonio said rang true. What was more, he had Sam for a witness. That Antonio should have traveled back the long distance from Celaya to murder Gonzalo seemed highly improbable. He had already won Gonzalo's money, honestly, as Sam could testify. Gonzalo had no valuables of any kind. Each of us knew the entire possessions of the others, and none of us could have secreted anything on his person, for we were all going around half naked. There remained no grounds for suspicion. Antonio was innocent.

"Well, my dear Antonio, you must accept my sincere apologies for thinking that you'd be guilty of Gonzalo's murder or responsible for his death."

"That's okay, Gales. No offense taken. But all the same, I wouldn't have thought that you'd have been so quick to suspect me. I've never given anyone cause to think badly of me, have I?"

"True, you haven't. But you know it was remarkable how all the circumstances pointed against you. You and Sam were the last with Gonzalo in the house. If, as you say, Gonzalo didn't go with you, he never left the house; he was murdered there. Mr. Shine told me that no one else had been around since you left. There's nothing to steal there, and there's no trail nearby that could lead anyone there by chance. I was up that way again because I had to wait for a message from the oil field. It was sheer curiosity that made me look inside the house, where I found Gonzalo dead. He had several knife wounds, the most serious of which was a stab in the chest from which he'd evidently bled to death."

As I went on describing the wounds, a terrible change came over Antonio. He turned as white as a sheet, stared at me with horrified eyes, moved his lips, and gulped again and again. But no words came. With his left hand he worked at his face and about his throat as though he wanted to tear the flesh away, while with his right hand he groped toward my shoulder and my chest as if he were trying to discover if there really were someone sitting beside him or if it were only a figment of his imagination, a dream from which he would awake.

I was at a loss to know what to make of it. It just didn't make sense. Antonio had suddenly taken on the appearance of a guilty man who had just begun to realize the full implications of his dark deed. And only a few moments before he'd been laughing at the thought that I suspected him of Gonzalo's murder. How was I to figure out his behavior? And yet I must; otherwise I'd get lost in my own confused thoughts. I might even begin to imagine that I'd killed Gonzalo myself!

The park lights came on. Night had suddenly closed in

around us. Darkness had fallen within the moments since the start of Antonio's inner battle, for I'd last seen his face, open and guileless, in clear sunset light. Then the coming of night had obscured what I'd glimpsed of the true, the undisguised Antonio. What should have been for me the unforgettable experience of studying the features of a man assailed by the powers of darkness, shaken, moved, his every hair and every pore electrified, was now distorted by the harsh lights. They lied, throwing lines and shadows into Antonio's face that were in truth not there.

But his warm breath was truth, his groping, clawing fingers were truth. All the rest was footlights.

An Indian laborer was sitting on a bench near us, ragged like tens of thousands of others of his class because their wages are barely sufficient to pay for their food. It often happened that such a laborer had nothing left over for a thirty-centavo bunk in one of the many flophouses—dormitorios, they're called— where in the morning fifty or eighty or a hundred bedfellows of every race and every nation, afflicted with every disease in the medical dictionary as well as others that no doctor had heard about as yet, all washed in the same bowl, all dried themselves on the same towel, and combed themselves with the same comb.

The Indian had fallen asleep on the bench. His limbs sagged and his overworked, exhausted body was crumpled into a heap of rags.

At this moment a policeman came sneaking up. He circled the bench, his eyes glued on the man sleeping there. Then, when he was again behind the bench, he raised his leather whip and brought it down hard and pitilessly on the shoulder of the sleeping man, at the same time yelling at him: "You bum, you, get up, out of here or I'll turn you in! The law prohibits sleeping in the park and you know it. Get going before I get seriously rough with you."

With a suppressed groan the Indian plunged forward as if a sword had slashed into him. Then his body jerked upward again and, writhing and moaning, he felt for his tortured shoulder. The policeman now stepped in front of him and grinned maliciously. Great tears of pain streamed down the Indian's face. But he said nothing. He didn't get up. He remained sitting where he was, for he like any other citizen was entitled to his park seat. No one could deny his right to sit on the bench, however ragged he might be and however many elegant caballeros and señoritas might be strolling about to enjoy the cool of the evening and listen to the bandstand music.

Yes, the Indian knew that he was a citizen of a free country, where a millionaire had no more right to occupy a park bench than a penniless native. The Indian could have sat there for twenty-four hours if he'd wanted to, but sleeping on a park bench wasn't permitted. Freedom didn't go that far, though the bench was in Freedom Square. Locally, it was the sort of freedom in which anyone in authority could whip anyone not in authority: the age-old antagonism between two worlds, almost as old as the story of the expulsion from Paradise; the age-old antagonism between the police and the weary, burdened ones, the tired and hungry. The Indian had been in the wrong and he knew it; that was why he said nothing but only moaned. Satan or Gabriel—this policeman regarded himself as the latter—was in the right.

No! He wasn't in the right! No! No! The blood rushed to my head. In England, Germany, the U.S.A., everywhere it is the police who do the whipping and the one in rags who gets whipped. And then the people who sit smugly at their well-laden tables are surprised when someone rocks the table, overturns it, and shatters everything to fragments. A bullet wound heals. A cut with a whip never heals. It eats ever more deeply into the flesh, reaches the heart and finally the brain, releasing a cry to make the very earth tremble, a cry of "Revenge!" Why is Russia in the hands of the bolshies? Because the Russians were a people most whipped before the rise of the new era. The policeman's whip or club prepares the way for an offensive that makes continents quiver and political systems explode.

Woe to the complacent and smug when the whipped cry "Revenge!" Woe to the satiated when the welts of lashes eat into the hearts of the hungry and turn the minds of the long-suffering! I was forced to become a rebel and a revolutionary, a revolutionary out of love of justice, out of a desire to help the wretched and the ragged. The sight of injustice and cruelty makes as many revolutionaries as do privation and hunger.

I leaped to my feet and got over to the bench where the policeman was still standing, drawing his whip through his hand, slashing it through the air, grinning bright-eyed at his writhing victim. He took no notice of me. Obviously he thought that I was just going to sit down on the bench.

But I went right up to him and said: "Take me to the police station at once. I'm going to report you. Your instructions only give you the right to use the whip if you are attacked, or in a street riot after you've given warning. You must know that."

"But the dog was asleep on the bench here." The little devil of a cop scarcely taller than five feet, was trying to defend himself.

"You could have awakened him and told him that he shouldn't sleep here, and if he fell asleep again you could then have turned him off the bench, but under no circumstances should you strike him. So come along with me to the station. By tomorrow you won't have a chance to whip anyone."

The little cop eyed me for a moment, took note that I was a

white man, and realized that I was in earnest. He hung his whip onto the hook of his belt, and with one lightning leap disappeared as if the earth had swallowed him.

The Indian, without a word, disappeared into the night. I walked slowly back to where I had left Antonio. What now, when I see him again?

What is murder? I thought. It all comes to the same thing, the law of the jungle. The whole world is a jungle. Eat or be eaten! The fly by the spider, the spider by the bird, the bird by the snake—so it went, round and round. Until there came a world disaster, or a revolution; and the whole circle would begin again, only the other way around.

Antonio, you were right! You are right! The living are always right! It is the dead who are guilty. If you hadn't murdered Gonzalo, he'd have murdered you. Perhaps. No, certainly. It's the law of the jungle. You pick it up so quickly in the bush. It's all around you and, after all, is only the natural result of an outstanding capacity for imitation.

10

 "No," said Antonio, calmer now, "I certainly didn't mean to kill Gonzalo. It might just as well have been me. Believe me, amigo mio! I'm not to blame for his death."

"I know, Antonio. It might just as well have been you. It's the bush that grabs us all by the scruff of the neck and has us at its mercy."

"Yes! You're right, Gales, it's the bush. Here in town we'd never have hit on such a crazy idea. But the bush talks to you the whole night through: a jungle pheasant giving his death cry as he's attacked, a cougar howling as he goes to the kill; nothing but blood and strife. In the bush it's teeth; with us it was knives. But, honestly, it was only a game! We did it for fun—really, only fun, nothing more.

"We used knives, but it might just as well have been dice, or cards, or a roulette wheel. The point was that after seven weeks' work we didn't have enough money left to get away from that godforsaken place to look for something better. We had just about the same amount. Gonzalo had a little over twenty pesos. I had twenty-five.

"It was Sunday night. We wanted to be on our way on

Monday morning. Charley had left a few days before; Abraham had gone too. That left the three of us, Gonzalo, Sam, and me.

"We counted out our money on the floor. Each of us had some gold pieces, and the small change in silver. And as the money lay there before us, hardly visible in the light of the fire, Gonzalo let fly.

" 'What can I do with these few lousy coppers?' he asked. 'Here we've been, slaving away like mad for seven long weeks, seven days a week, from dawn to sundown, all through the blazing heat. We limped home so done in we could hardly move our fingers to cook our miserable grub that we were too tired to swallow. We slept on the floor. No Sunday, no pleasure, no music, no dancing, no girls, no drinking—only some stinking tobacco rolled in corn husks. And now look—what's the use of these lousy coppers?'

"He shoved the money away with his foot.

" 'My shirt is in rags,' he grumbled on. 'My pants are rags. My sandals—take a look at them, Antonio—no soles, no nothing. In the end, after sweating like a work horse, there's nothing left. If only it were forty pesos!'

"Saying this, his face lit up.

" 'With forty pesos I could manage. I could go to Mexico City, buy myself some decent clothes so that if I wanted to say buenas tardes to a girl she'd see me as a human being. And I'd still have a few pesos to tide me over for a few days.'

" 'You're right, Gonzalo,' I said, 'forty pesos is just the sum I need to buy the absolute necessities.'

" 'Do you know what I'm thinking?' Gonzalo went on. 'Let's play for the money. Neither of us can get anywhere with the few sickly coppers we've got. If you get my money or I get yours, then at least one of us can do something. As it is, we're both bums. I'd drink away these few coppers at one sitting, just out of rage at having worked for nothing.'

"Gonzalo's idea wasn't bad," Antonio went on with his tale. "I too would have drunk up the little I had left. Once you get started on that goddamned tequila, you don't stop until the last centavo's gone. You go on drinking, drunk or sober; and what you don't get down your gullet, your fellow boozers will swig for you. The café and flophouse keepers will cheat a drunk, and the miserable coins that are left are pinched from your pocket. You know all about it, Gales."

Didn't I, though. I knew cheap tequila. You shudder after each copita and have to gulp down something for a chaser. The barkeeper, or cantinero, is always wise enough to keep a supply of pickled botanas on sticks, but they burn your throat. So you keep on guzzling tequila, drenching your gizzard with the stuff as if bewitched or as if the damned throat-stripper were some magic elixir which, for some mysterious reason, had to be shot down without touching the tongue. And when at last you think you've had enough, you've ceased to exist. Everything is wiped away—trouble, sorrow, anger, passion. Only absolute nothingness remains. World and ego are dispersed.

Antonio brooded for a while, as though searching his memory. Then he went on: "We had no cards and no dice. We drew sticks. But the same stake of one peso kept passing from one to the other. It was never more than five pesos that changed hands. Then we played heads or tails. Strange, it still was never more than a few pesos that passed from one pocket to the other. Sam played too, and his money didn't change much either. Meanwhile it had got late—ten or eleven o'clock by my judgment.

"Then Gonzalo got wild and cursed like a madman. He'd had enough of this kid's game, he said, and wanted to know for sure how he'd stand in the morning.

" 'Well, Gonzalo, what do you say we ought to do?'

" 'I don't know,' he said. 'That's just what makes me so mad.

Here we are fooling around like half-witted kids and not getting anywhere—back and forth all the time. It's enough to drive you up the pole.'

"Then, after squatting by the fire for a while, staring into the embers, rolling himself one cigarette after another and throwing them into the fire half smoked, he jumped up suddenly and said, 'I know what we'll do. We'll have an Aztec duel for the whole stake.'

" 'An Aztec duel?' I asked. 'What's that?'

" 'What? You don't know the Aztec duel?' Gonzalo was genuinely surprised.

" 'No. How should I, Gonzalo? My family is of Spanish descent, even if we have been here for more than a hundred years. I've never heard of an Aztec duel.'

" 'It's quite simple, Antonio. We take two young, straight saplings, trim them clean, tie our knives securely to the tips, and then hurl them at each other, until one or the other of us gives up from exhaustion. One of us will tire before the other; the one who stays on his feet wins, and gets the money. That will decide the money.'

"I thought it over for a few moments. It seemed a crazy idea to me.

" 'You're not scared by any chance, are you, Spaniard?' laughed Gonzalo.

"There was a funny sort of sneer in his voice and this made me flare up: 'Scared of you? Of an Indian? A Spaniard is never scared! I'll show you! Come on, let's have your Aztec duel!'

"We took a flaming stick from the fire and stumbled around in the bush until we'd found two suitable saplings. Sam had been directed to bring plenty of fuel and build up a good fire so that we could see where we were aiming. We stripped the saplings and tied our opened pocketknives firmly to their tips.

" 'We don't let the whole blade stick out,' said Gonzalo. 'We don't want to murder each other. It's only a game. The blade needn't stick out more than an inch. There, that's right!' he said, looking at my spear. 'Now we must bind a piece of heavy wood near the blade end to give the spear its proper shaft weight; otherwise it'll wobble and won't fly straight.'

"Then we padded our left arms with grass and wrapped them round with a coarse convas sack. 'This is important,' Gonzalo explained. 'That's where the fun comes in, catching and parrying the spear. The well-padded arm serves as a shield did in ancient times. You know, the old Aztec warriors also used shields. You must understand, in this duel we are fighting, that we don't want to kill one another, only exhaust the other partner. Keep all this in mind; it is supposed to be only a game.'

"When we'd got everything ready, Sam said: 'What about me? Am I supposed to stand by and watch? I want to be in on it too.'

"The Chink was right. He had to have something for his trouble as stakeholder and witness. You know what devils the Chinese are for gambling, don't you, Gales? They'd gamble away the price of their own funeral if given the chance.

" 'Now see here, Sam,' Gonzalo said to the Chink, 'you can bet on one of us.'

" 'Good,' Sam said. 'I'll bet on you, Gonzalo, five pesos. You give me five pesos if you win. If you lose, you get five pesos flom me. It's not in youl intelest to lose, because that would mean good-bye to youl twenty pesos.'

"We each deposited our twenty pesos, which Sam placed before him on a stone; then he added his own stake of five pesos. Sam paced off twenty-five steps from either side of the fire, and we each placed a wooden pole on the marks. If either duelist overstepped his mark he would forfeit five pesos to the other.

"Then we started throwing the spears at each other, parrying each spear with our grass-girded arm as it came to us, and then returning it. With the fire flickering and smoking as it was I could see Gonzalo only in uncertain outline. I could hardly see the spear as it flew toward me, the night was so pitch dark. At the second throw I got a stab in my right shoulder. You can still see the wound, Gales."

He pulled his shirt from his shoulder and I saw the stab wound, still not healed.

"Gradually, we got into our stride, or, rather, we got worked up. After a few more exchanges I got another stab which went through my trousers and into my leg. But I was a long way from finished.

"How long we kept on throwing, I don't know. As neither of us would give in, the tempo became more and more wild. An element of savagery entered into the match, and anybody watching us then never would have believed that it was only a game.

"Perhaps we threw for half an hour, perhaps for an hour; I don't know. Neither did I know if I'd hit Gonzalo at all seriously. But I knew that I was beginning to tire. The spear began to feel as if it weighed twenty pounds, and my throwing slowed down. Before long I found myself hardly able to bend down to pick up the spear, and once when I was bending I almost collapsed. But I knew that I mustn't allow myself to sink to the ground; if I did I would certainly be unable to get on my feet again.

"I couldn't see Gonzalo now. I couldn't see anything at all. I kept throwing the spears in the direction where I figured he must be. I no longer cared whether I hit him or not. All that worried me was that I shouldn't be the first to stop. So, as the spears kept coming from the other side, I kept throwing them back.

"Suddenly, as the fire flared up for an instant, I saw Gonzalo turning around to look for the spear, which evidently had missed him widely. He went back a few steps, found it, picked it up, and then, as he turned toward me to throw it, fell on his knees as heavily as if someone had knocked him down with a terrific blow.

"I didn't throw the spear which I had in my hand because I was only too glad to stand it upright and lean on it; otherwise I'd have dropped to the ground. If Gonzalo had gotten to his feet and thrown his spear, I couldn't have lifted my arm to ward it off or to throw it back.

"But Gonzalo remained on his knees. Sam ran to him and called out: 'Thel', now, I've lost my five pesos. Antonio, you've won. Gonzalo's given up.'

"I dragged myself to a box near the fire, but hadn't the strength to sit down on it. I dropped to the ground by the side of it. Sam dragged Gonzalo to the fire and gave him some water, which he gulped down.

"I now saw that his chest was covered with blood. But I was past being interested in anything around me. My head dropped, and as I opened my eyes I saw that my chest was as streaked with blood as Gonzalo's. But I didn't care. Nothing seemed to matter.

"Sam brought me the forty pesos and stuffed them into my pocket. I saw him also put five pesos into Gonzalo's pocket. I had the feeling that all this was happening a long way off.

"We stayed like this for a good half hour, maybe a whole hour. The fire died down.

"Then Sam said, 'I'm going to lie down and get some lest.'

"I echoed these words, as they were my own: 'Yes, I'm going to lie down and get some rest.'

"I saw Gonzalo get up, too, and staggering and clutching like me, he clambered up the ladder and into the house.

"When I'd dropped to the floor and just as I was dozing off, I heard Gonzalo say: 'If you leave early in the morning and I'm not up, don't bother to wake me. I want to get a good long sleep. I'm beat. Anyway, I can't travel with you on the train; I haven't got the fare.'

"Before dawn, Sam gave me a nudge. It was time to be off. We had to be at the station by eight o'clock that evening; otherwise we'd lose two days. It was still pitch dark. I could see nothing in the hut, not even Gonzalo. We didn't wake him but let him sleep undisturbed, and, picking up our bundles, were off just as dawn was breaking.

"A short distance from the house we met the Indian who wanted to buy Abraham's chickens.

"Well, there you are, Gales, that's the story, the true story."

"Antonio, you'd never have gotten Gonzalo to wake up that morning," I said.

"I've told you the true story, Gales. We can go and check it with Sam right now. He knows the truth."

"It's not necessary to check it, Antonio. Let's leave it at that. I believe you. I know the truth when I hear it."

The music in the bandshell started up.

I closed my eyes. I wanted to shut out the harsh electric lights. I saw Gonzalo lying on the floor, banished from the world of the living and the hopeful, his hand clasping to his breast a ball of raw, blood-blackened cotton.

Cotton.

Antonio evidently had been watching me without my being aware of it.

"Why are you weeping, Gales?"

"Shut up! You . . . you must be seeing things. You do get some crazy ideas into your head."

He was silent.

"This damned funeral music, Antonio! Why can't they play 'The Merry Widow' or 'Yes, we have no bananas'! Life is fun! Funeral marches are for corpses, comic opera for the living. Come on, Antonio. It's nearly ten. What did that son-of-a-bitch say? 'Be to work on time,' he said, for one peso twenty-five the day!"

Book Two

11

The owner of the Aurora Bakery, Señor Doux, always looked miserable, as if he were suffering from chronic malaria. He was off-color and went about his business like someone mortally sick. But in truth he was an active, hearty man; he could at one sitting eat enough for twelve strong men. He got up at four in the morning and breakfasted on a quart of milk and six fried eggs with ham. Then he had a good-sized glass of brandy and went off to the market for the day's supplies. Apart from the bakery and pastry shop he had a flourishing café, where, in addition to the usual iced drinks, soda pop, ice creams, wine, and beer, you could get breakfast, the comida lunch of the day, and supper. The bakery and café were on the ground floor of Doux's two-story building. Above them there was also a hotel, but it was not run by Doux; he sublet it, and every day he had some stimulating conversation with his tenant. You only had to overhear this conversation to understand why Doux always looked so very yellowish green in the jowls.

The usual subject of the argument was water. In the tropics water is not only one of the most precious of all things, it is also the object of continual strife. Nature fights for water as a matter of life and death; animals tear each other to pieces for water, or so forbear on its account that the jaguar will not harm the doe at the water's edge but lies in wait at a respectful distance for its return.

The struggle of plants and trees for water has a gentleness. But when human beings fight over water they outdo in cunning savagery all other earthly creatures.

Doux's building was constructed, in the Latin-American colonial style, around a quadrangle, in which lush tropical plants grew, some of them to a height above that of the upper floor. The café occupied the front portion of the ground floor; the right wing contained the kitchen and storerooms; the left housed the bakery and pastry shop, as well as the dormitory of the bakery workers. The rear section was the proprietor's residence.

The hotel section, all of the upper floor, extended in a rectangle over the courtyard, with all rooms opening onto a continuous balcony looking into the greenery. The rooms on the street side of the hotel opened also onto a second balcony that ran along the whole front of the building.

On the roof were two large water tanks, each served by a separate well. One was for the lower floor, the other for the upper. Each had its own motor-driven pump. When the dry season came, the well for the bakery and café ran dry, but the hotel well had ample water. The café and bakery couldn't operate without water, and that was where the fun started. Señor Doux wanted to pump the water from the hotel tank into his tank, maintaining that, after all, he was the owner of both wells. His tenant, however, didn't concede this; it was in his contract that the hotel tank was at his exclusive disposal. He was afraid that if he let the café take water from his tank, he might some day find himself without water, and thus be obliged to deny his guests the privilege of baths. A hotelkeeper in the tropics who has to refuse baths might just as well close up his hotel.

Both tanks were covered and padlocked; the tenant had a key for his, and Señor Doux had a key for the café tank. Doux therefore had no alternative but to force the lock of his tenant's tank at night, lower a hose into the tank, connect the hose to his own pump, and start it running. The tenant was usually awakened by the sound of the pump, and so pandemonium broke out in the middle of the night. The hotel guests joined in; so did the café clients, who were often flushed with drink and ready to pick a fight and take sides. Bottles, chairs, loaves of bread, chunks of ice, and horrible curses and maledictions came flying through the air. Meanwhile, the pump was neutral and indifferent to the uproar as it went to work and filled Señor Doux's tank. At that point, Doux shut off the pump, retracted the hose, and peace reigned once more—until morning, when the tenant would take measures to secure the hotel tank for the night. These measures were always in some way undone by Señor Doux.

One morning the hotel tenant sent for a carpenter and instructed him to barricade the tank. Now Señor Doux ran to the police, for the building was his property and it was against the law for the tenant to build barricades on Doux's roof. So during the night the tank was forced again, because Señor Doux's establishment just had to have water.

There were, therefore, good and sufficient reasons for Señor Doux's ghastly appearance and tremendous appetite. His first breakfast was followed by a better one at six, when he returned from his marketing. Now he had fish, roast beef, a half bottle of wine, and three or four slices of cake.

Meanwhile the first customers of the day were coming in; suppliers had to be bargained with and their accounts settled; the mail arrived. Then came the buyers for the baked goods, each making up his selection of bread, rolls, cakes, pastries, biscuits, and candied fruits.

At half past eight Señor Doux had what he called a regular breakfast, at which his wife joined him. This time there was an egg dish, two meat dishes, beer, and a large dessert, followed by coffee, with plenty of cream of course.

Señora Doux had the features of a pretty woman, but was more than plump. In contradiction to the idea that fat people are always jolly, Señora Doux was perpetually bad tempered. When exceptionally heavy orders for cakes and pastries came in, a faint smile appeared on her face, but it lasted for only a few seconds. The café might be full to the bursting point and customers fighting for seats, but Señora Doux would wear her sour expression and look at every new arrival as if he had done her a personal injury that increased the misery of her life. She never wore shoes, but always soft, felt slippers. She never went out—that is, I never saw her go out—for she was afraid that one of the waiters might steal money or food in her absence. Her eyes went everywhere; nothing happened in the place that she didn't know about, or over which she had no control.

The thing she regretted most (actually she regretted everything) was that people, or at any rate she herself, had to sleep; for while she slept, something might happen that she couldn't know about. For this reason she regarded no one with greater mistrust than the workers in the bakery. They worked during the night hours when Señora Doux just had to get some sleep in order to be able to supervise the café throughout the day and evening. Even so, she stayed up late into the night.

Señora Doux also took care of the cash till. Even if she could have brought herself to hire a señorita for the job, no cashier would have worked with her for long. The señorita might be as honest as the archangel with the sword, but Señora Doux still would have accused her several times a day of embezzling a few pesos.

It was a difficult business with the till. Señora Doux didn't trust any waiter. She sat at the cash counter or wandered around the place observing what the guests were eating. When they paid, the waiter had to hand over the money at once. The Señora reasoned that if waiters were allowed to pocket the money they collected, amounting at times to hundreds of pesos, and to settle up at the end of the shift, there was nothing to prevent them from leaving hat and coat behind and walking off with the cash a quarter of an hour before quitting time. It must be admitted that such things happened, even when the waiter had collected only sixty or seventy pesos, but in the Café Aurora such a thing wasn't possible.

On days when bakery orders were slack, the bakers and confectioners had a rough time. Señora Doux would intentionally order them around in such a way that one or another among them would ask for his money and leave, for on slack days she regarded the bakery expenses as so much wasted money. If on the following day the orders doubled or trebled, the men had to work three, four, or five hours more, since of course no new worker had been hired to replace the one who had quit.

The musicians in the café fared no better; in fact, worse. The bakers at least produced something; but in the minds of the Señor and Señora music was the most absurd waste of money imaginable. However, the neighboring cafés had music, so the Café Aurora had to have music too, if it was to stay in business. Señor Doux had a row with the orchestra every day. If the place was empty he told the musicians it was their fault because they played so badly. Sometimes, after such a row, the musicians packed up their instruments, asked for their money, and left. Señora Doux was well satisfied with this state of affairs as it enabled her to save money, and, besides, she could explain to the guests that the musicians had quit.

But after a few days the customers would get restless and

demand music, so Señor Doux would have to run and look for musicians. On such occasions it might happen that he could get only one guitarist, and the customers would stay away until a good orchestra was hired. After a while there would be another row and the whole story would be repeated.

One day an excellent eight-piece orchestra arrived from Mexico City and offered its services to the various cafés, coming first to Doux in the Aurora.

"Fifty pesos a day for eight men? I'm not going to pay that! And their meals in the bargain? I'm not crazy. And contracted by the week, with three days' notice? You can go all around this town and you won't find any café owner crazy enough to take you on those terms. I'll pay you twenty-five, on a daily basis. I can get musicians enough when I want them, on a day's notice."

So the orchestra went to another café and got what they asked for. As a result, that café was full of customers every night, despite the fact that people in this region don't sit around at café tables or loaf in restaurants. Here, they usually stay just long enough to swallow their ice creams or sip their refresco drinks, and then they go. They prefer to promenade in the parks and squares, or to sit there on the benches rather than at café tables. But the music could hold customers for another iced drink or an extra bottle of beer, and that all the more readily since the café owner was decent enough not to put a surcharge on the drinks because of the musical entertainment.

The café where the new orchestra played to such crowds was only five doors away from the Aurora, and the Aurora was as empty as a coffin in a carpenter's shop. The Señora wanted to turn off half the lights because they were burning unnecessarily, but her husband woudn't hear of it. Every hour he strolled over to the cinema without hat or jacket, ostensibly to look at the posters of the coming attractions. Actually he went to count the customers in the Moderna. He passed the competing café seemingly without turning his head, but in fact he saw every guest in the Moderna, and to his chagrin he saw many of his former clients.

For a few days he put up with it. Then he posted himself in front of his café and waited for the first violinist of the Moderna orchestra to come along.

"One moment, señor!"

"Yes?"

"Wouldn't you like to come and play here? I'll pay you fifty."

"I'm sorry, we're getting sixty-five."

"That I won't pay."

"Muy bien, señor, adios."

After a week had passed, he asked the first violinist once more: "All right, for fifty, señor."

"Settled. Agreed. From Friday, then."

Señor Doux rushed in to his wife. "I've got the orchestra. For fifty!"

The orchestra had agreed to play for fifty because they had been given notice at the Moderna and had no other engagement in town. They were no longer a novelty and the customers were ready for something different.

The cream had been skimmed off. The Café Aurora was full enough, but not as full as the Moderna had been every night. So Señor Doux told the orchestra that they played abominably. The musicians wouldn't take this, it led to a row, and they left the café; therefore Señor Doux didn't have to pay "notice" wages, and so saved money once again.

At about half past eleven every morning, Señor Doux was finished with his account books and ready to sit down to lunch. At ten, unable to hold out until noon, he would eat a cold chicken; but now he had his first proper meal of the day.

Then he took a siesta. At five he got up, washed and shaved, and, driven by hunger, hurried into the café.

He stayed in the café until closing time. The local police weren't concerned with the moral behavior of the towns-people; they left that to the people themselves. Anyone who had the money and time to hang about all night in a café was free to do so; it was his money, his time, and his health. When the place was empty the landlord would close up, if he pleased, without the advice or penalties of the police. And as there was no official closing time, no one got any satisfaction out of defying regulations; thus at midnight the cafés were so empty that it hardly paid to keep the lights on. The people who for professional reasons had to be up all night didn't frequent the cafés, but were to be found in the bars, which served full meals or specialty dishes at all hours of the day and night, and were cheaper than the cafés.

No matter how quiet the café was, we in the bakery were having our busiest time at midnight.

"You can clean up the baking sheets," the master baker told me. "You'll be able to do that all right. If the old girl comes in," he said, referring to Señora Doux, who was barely thirty, "just keep on cleaning baking tins. She has to poke her nose into everything, but if you're busy she won't notice that you don't know the trade. She won't come down here now, though, because the old man's up there with her, and they don't often get around to wasting time on that! It beats me that they find any time or thought for it at all, but I don't suppose their minds are really on it while they're at it. They're more likely to be thinking about us and wondering if we're beating up an egg or two for ourselves. Good idea. We'll do it now."

He took some eggs, broke them in businesslike fashion, gave them a quick whisk, added some butter, and popped them into the oven, producing a baked omelet. After we finished it off, I learned how to clean the baking sheets. It wasn't as simple as it sounds, but something that had to be learned properly. Then I had to weigh off flour, which must be done exactly. Then I had to break five hundred eggs and separate the yolks from the whites. If you went about this in mother's way, it would take a week; here, I had to break and separate the five hundred eggs in about twenty minutes, and if the slightest trace of yolk got into the whites there would be culinary complications.

Later I learned to look after the dough-mixing machines, keep the oven fires going, set the dough for bread and rolls, ice the small cakes, cut the flan puddings and prepare them for decoration, wash the pots and pans, wipe off the tables, sweep the bakehouse, crush the sugar for the icing, prepare the icing, and do many other things. I learned them all bit by bit; that way, one can learn anything. There's absolutely nothing that you can't learn if you go about it one step at a time.

Saturday arrived—pay day. But there was no pay. "Mañana, tomorrow," said Señor Doux. Sunday was the busiest day of the week, but when it came to paying wages, Señor Doux explained that he never paid wages on Sunday. "Mañana." But on Monday he didn't pay because he hadn't been to the bank. On Tuesday there wasn't enough money in the till because he had spent the money he'd brought from the bank for supplies. On Wednesday, the waiters got paid first; on Thursday he had no money on hand and couldn't pay the bakers. On Friday he couldn't be found; whenever anyone went to look for him they were told he'd just gone to his flat and didn't want to be disturbed. By Saturday two weeks' wages were due, but then his outgo was so heavy because he had to buy supplies for Sunday, "the busiest day," and besides this the banks closed at noon on Saturday. "Mañana," he said; but tomorrow was Sunday, and he never paid wages on Sundays. "Mañana," he recited; but on Monday he didn't go to the bank. And so it went on.

I had been there three weeks when I got my first pay; and then I was paid not for three weeks but for one week. It went on and on like this, with Señor Doux always being weeks and weeks in arrears with the wages. But we couldn't be fifteen minutes behind in our work; if we were, there was hell to pay, for customers expected their bread and pastries on the dot, like clockwork. We had to put in fifteen, sixteen hours a day, and sometimes as many as twenty-one. Señor Doux took this for granted; he also took it for granted that he paid wages when it suited him, and not when they fell due.

The master baker had four months' wages owing him. He couldn't have left the place even if he'd wanted to, for Doux would have taken months to pay off the balance. As for the rest of us, there was no other work to be found, and even if there had been, we had no time to go and look for it. By the time we'd finished in the bakehouse it was usually late afternoon and often evening, and places of work where we might have inquired for a job were already closed. We just had to stick it out at the Aurora. If you want to live you have to eat, and if you can't find food any other way you have to fall in line with the man who has the food.

The waiters were no better off. They received only twenty pesos a month and were expected to live on their tips. But the people weren't liberal with tips; and when customers were few and far between, the waiters had an even harder time. Then, too, they were blamed for the shortage of customers and Señora Doux begrudged them even their twenty pesos in wages. The bakers lived in the dormitory, but the waiters had families and lived at home, so that they had household expenses. They weren't even given food, but got a meal only occasionally as a favor or special privilege.

One of the waiters got the fever and was dead in three days; he was a Spaniard who had come over here only two years before. A Mexican called Morales came to take his place, a quick, intelligent fellow. When I had to take pastries into the café I would notice that Morales was usually talking to one or another of his fellow waiters. Of course they always talked among themselves when they weren't serving customers, but now I saw a difference. Before, the waiters had talked together superficially, about the lotteries or about their side activities or about girls or about their families. They had laughed and joked as they gossiped.

But when Morales spoke with them it wasn't a laughing matter, and they listened to him attentively. Morales always did the talking and the others always listened. I saw something come to life: the Union of Restaurant Employees.

The Mexican trade unions had no cumbersome bureaucratic machinery. Their secretaries didn't consider themselves to be "officials," but were actually young hotheaded revolutionaries. The Mexican unions had come into being during the 1910–1920 Revolution, and had developed along the most modern lines. They could draw upon the experiences of the North-American trade unions and of the Russian Revolution; they had the explosive power of a young Sturm und Drang movement, and the elasticity of an organization that is still feeling its way and changing its tactics daily.

Up the street at the Moderna there was a waiters' strike. Doux, however, smiled to himself, having no fear of such a thing happening in his place. And now all the Moderna's customers were coming to Doux's Café Aurora because they were ill at ease in the strike-bound Moderna. They had good reason to be, for the police were neutral in the struggles of striking workers. If a customer went into a strike-bound café and got hit on the head with a flying brick or a bottle, he would be helped to the Red Cross station to get his wound dressed, but aside from that the police wouldn't worry about him. After all, the pickets in front of the café had warned him of the strike; he had read of it in the newspapers and had had enough handbills thrust at him, so that he might have known what to expect. There was no need for him to go into this café; he could have gone to another one, or taken a seat in the plaza, or gone for a promenade. Anyone who deliberately enters a place where stones are being thrown has only himself to blame if he gets one on the head.

After four days of strike, the Moderna agreed to all the union's demands.

12

 One afternoon, about three weeks after the Moderna strike was settled, when there were only a few customers in the café, Morales went to Doux and said: "Now listen, señor, an eight-hour day, twelve pesos a week, one full meal a day, and coffee and rolls twice a day."

For a moment Doux looked scared, but he quickly collected himself and said: "Come along to the cashier's counter, Morales. There are your wages, you may go. You're dismissed, fired!"

Morales turned around, took off his white jacket, and picked up the money that Doux had set down on the counter. All the other waiters, who had been watching, immediately took off their jackets and went up to the counter. Taken aback, Doux paid them their wages and let the men go; he was quite sure that he could get other men right away.

In his anger Doux had roughly pushed his wife's nose out of the till, almost knocking her off her tall stool. With everything having happened so suddenly, Señora Doux had looked on speechless, for once.

"What happened?" she now managed excitedly to ask. "Why did you pay them?"

"Imagine asking me to double their wages and shorten their hours! I fired them without even listening to all the further demands they had in store for us."

At this explanation, Señora Doux calmed down. "That was the most sensible thing, cheri, you have ever done in your life. We have been overpaying them wastefully anyway since the day we were fools enough to get into business in this godforsaken country where everybody seems to be going crazy with what they call their Revolution. The ones you fired were Bolsheviks anyway. They were thieves on top of that, never turning in the exact amount they received from the customers."

"Now don't you worry, cherie. In a few hours we'll get more waiters than we need. They're running around falling over their own feet in their eagerness to land a job."

Señora Doux finished serving the few customers. When new customers arrived and saw that there were no waiters they did not even sit down but left at once. A few foreigners came in, ordered something, and thought the slow service was a local peculiarity.

The following day there were pickets outside the café and handbills were distributed with great gusto. Any person now wanting to enter had to confront the pickets, but everything was quite calm; there was no sign of violence. There were no police around.

Aside from a few of Doux's regular customers, only foreigners went in. They couldn't read the handbills and hadn't understood what the pickets had said to them. The pickets, of course, didn't bother the foreigners, who were mostly North American, English, or French and who, soon feeling the atmosphere to be depressing, quickly left the place, some of them without touching the food or drink they had ordered.

To Señora Doux's chagrin, waiters were not falling over themselves to get a job. Finally, after two days, Doux found two, one an Italian, the other a Yugoslav; both were in rags, pitiful specimens. Doux gave them white jackets, shirt fronts and collars, and black bow ties, but no pants or shoes, and it was in the lower departments where the two fellows looked the most deplorable. They couldn't understand a word of Spanish and were quite useless as waiters; but Doux wanted them there only to spike the guns of the pickets, so to speak.

In the evening at about half past eight the Italian was standing at one of the doors, all of which were wide open so that you could see from the outside everything that happened inside, as clearly as if it were happening in the middle of the street. That was the local way, for the customers liked to look out and liked to be seen, just as the passers-by enjoyed looking in and seeing people having a pleasant time in a café.

The Italian stood at the door and flapped his napkin, proud of being a waiter; in normal circumstances he might perhaps have been a good dishwasher. The pickets took little notice of him, merely casting a glance in his direction now and then.

Before long, a young fellow came along with a heavy wooden stick in his hand. The proud new waiter instinctively took a step backward; but the young man mounted the doorstep and struck him two sound blows on the head. Then he threw the stick down and casually walked away.

The waiter fell headlong, bleeding profusely from the wound on his head. Doux rushed to the door calling "Police! Police!" A policeman appeared, swinging his truncheon. The few customers in the café quickly left the place.

"They've killed him!" shouted Doux.

"Who did?" asked the policeman.

"I don't know," answered Doux, "probably those waiters who are on strike."

Two of the pickets immediately sprang forward and shouted: "If you say that again, you son-of-a-bitch, we'll break every bone in your body."

Señor Doux quickly retreated into the café and said no more.

"Did you see who struck this man here?" a second policeman who had come up asked the pickets.

"Yes, I saw him," said one of the pickets. "A young fellow came up with a piece of wood—there, it's still lying there—and just hit out at him."

"Do you know the fellow?"

"No. He doesn't belong to our union."

"Then he had nothing to do with the strike. It's probably some other affair; perhaps some skirts involved."

"No doubt it is," the picket agreed.

The two policemen took the fallen waiter to the station, where he was bandaged up and kept overnight for his safety.

"Hey, you in there, yes, you, you dirty scab," the pickets called into the Yugoslav, "how long are you going to stay in there? You'll get one with an iron bar. We haven't got any more wood to spare."

As all this was said in Spanish, the Yugoslav didn't understand a word, but he sensed what was being said to him and, turning pale, he retreated to the back of the room.

Señor Doux had heard and of course understood. He ran to the door and again called for the police, but none came. A quarter of an hour passed. Then he saw a policeman standing on the corner and called him over.

"The pickets have threatened to kill my waiter!"

"Which one threatened to kill him?" asked the policeman.

"Him!" and Doux pointed to Morales, who hadn't made any threats, but who was most hated by Doux, of course.

"Did you threaten to kill the waiter?" asked the policeman.

"No, I didn't, and the thought would never occur to me," said Morales. "I wouldn't even speak to the dirty, stinking scab, dirty and stinking all over as hell."

"I can quite believe it," said the policeman. "Now, who did threaten to kill him?"

"I told him not to come too close to the door because something might unexpectedly drop on his head from the roof or the balcony and hurt him," said one of the pickets.

The policeman turned around to Señor Doux, who was standing in the doorway. "Now, listen here, señor, what do you mean by saying such things? They're simply not true."

"Well, they half killed the other waiter," Doux said defensively.

"You'd better make it up with your men," the policeman said. "Then things like this won't happen."

"A fine thing," bellowed Doux, "a man can't even get proper protection from the police any longer."

"Not so fast," said the policeman. "You'd better stop insulting the police force, or I might turn you in."

"I'm a taxpayer and I've got a right to get police protection."

"What have taxes to do with it?" the policeman interrupted. "The waiters pay taxes, too. Settle your affairs with your men and quit calling for the police."

The Yugoslav was standing hesitantly inside the café while this discussion was going on. Meanwhile a crowd of people had gathered, all of whom seemed to side with the waiters. It was partly their show of sympathy that had emboldened the policeman who was, after all, a wage earner himself. He could never be sure, however, that Doux hadn't a close friend among the police inspectors who might accuse him of neglecting his duty.

After the policeman left, the Yugoslav took off his white jacket and went over to the counter to get his day's pay. Señor Doux asked him what it was all about, why he wanted to leave. The man couldn't answer, but tried to explain with eloquent gestures that his buddy had got one over the head with a club and that he didn't want the same to happen to him. Outside, the pickets and passers-by were following the demonstration of primeval sign language with evident enjoyment. Doux tried to make the Yugoslav understand that he would be absolutely safe if he stayed in the café. But the poor man wouldn't accept Doux's assurance.

Had he been more familiar with the country's ways he would have known that he was safe at no time in any place, that he couldn't stay within four walls forever, and that all would be up with him the moment he walked out. For his face was already well known to every worker in town, and there was no need for a photograph or a poster. Even the four walls of the café were no shelter, for some day, the next day or the day after, somebody might walk into the café, give an order to him, and when he brought it give him such a blow on the head with a bottle that an ambulance would have to come and collect him. And before anyone in the café realized what had happened, the avenger would be several blocks away. No one, not even a star detective, would find him.

That is why there were few scabs in the Republic; it was well known that effective measures were taken against them. War is war, and the workers were determined to wage war until they had won not just one battle but the whole campaign. States at war permit themselves the use of any weapon, so why shouldn't the workers in their war? Workers usually make the mistake of wanting to be regarded as respectable citizens, but no one thinks the better of them for it.

Of course, Señor Doux cheated the Yugoslav out of his scab's pay, giving him only fifty centavos and charging him forty for a broken tumbler. After collecting his pay, he approached the doorway and looked out at the striking waiters. As he stood there in his shirtsleeves, which were little more than filthy rags, the pickets saw the wretched man for what he really was. When he finally took courage and came out of the café, one of the pickets promptly took him in charge, accompanied him to the union office, found him a place to stay for the night, and promised to get him a job in a tin works.

Something entirely different happened to the Italian. On the following morning he was brought before the Police Superintendent, who, instead of commending him for his loyal scabbing, asked to see his immigration certificate.

"I haven't got one," he answered through an interpreter.

"How did you get into this country?"

"On a ship."

"Oh, so you deserted from a ship."

"No, I was paid off."

"Oh, yes, we know all about that sort of paying off. So we're going to hand you over to your Consul with the understanding that he send you back to Italy on the next ship. You're a troublemaker, and we've no room for such as you here."

A police officer took him to the Consul who, from that moment, would be responsible for him and maintain him until he could be shipped back to his country.

"What sort of mischief have you been up to, stealing?" the Consul asked.

"No. I was working as a waiter in the Aurora until I got one over the head."

"But there's a strike on at the Aurora. Didn't you know that?"

"Sure. Otherwise I wouldn't have gotten the job as a waiter. I'm a carpenter, really."

"Look here, my man, this Republic has a workers' government. Scabs are not popular here. So you see your activities in this country have come to an end. And don't try to bolt out of here, for I'll catch you and have you arraigned. You're now under my authority; I've put up bail for you so that you won't have to wait in jail until you can be shipped home. The jails here are no joke, you know. They're a serious business, and at least you're saved from them. So behave yourself."

Two days later he was deported to the country of his origin on the grounds that he had entered the Republic illegally.

And that was how the matter of the scabs at the Aurora was settled.

There were a few loyal customers who continued to come to the café, and these were served by Doux and his wife; but that couldn't be called business. There was not much for us to do in the bakery either, apart from outside orders to be filled.

One afternoon there were six or eight customers in the place, including a police inspector called Lamas. He patronized the Aurora regularly, afternoons and evenings, and ran up quite a bill, which he was always going to pay "mañana." Although he was married and had two children, he also had two mistresses to support; thus he was always in debt. Now he sat among the guests who were having their ice creams and sipping their drinks; at one table a game of dominoes was in progress, at another one of cards.

In some countries pickets are respectable law-abiding citizens who believe in authority. They don't talk much, and when a policeman says, "Stand back! You're blocking traffic!" they move at once, as if the police paid them and not the other way around.

In Mexico, the workers were more or less undisciplined and the union secretaries were obliged to go along with the actions of the rank and file. The remarkable thing was that they won practically every strike.

"Hey, you," a picket called out to one of the customers, "don't eat that ice. It's only sugar and water, there's not a spoonful of cream in it. The pig wants to make as much out of your portion as he would if there were no strike."

But the customer, obviously a friend of Doux's, called out: "Are you paying for this ice or am I?—you dirty clod!"

"You'd better watch out, you filthy scab, that I don't get rid of you," said the picket, amid loud laughter from outside.

One of the customers had a lady with him who was drinking fruit juice through a straw. "Is she still a virgin?" another picket shouted in. "Hurry up, fellow, before some other man gets in first."

The lady went on sipping her drink as if she had heard nothing, but her escort shouted back: "Shut up, you son-of-a-bitch! It's none of your business."

At this point Doux went to the door and said: "You're not to annoy my guests. Shut up and leave my guests alone!"

"Guests? They're not guests. They're a lot of lousy pimps," shouted the pickets, joined by a group of youths who were hanging about. "Pay a decent wage and give proper food, or we'll tear the hide off you. And you'd better be quick about it, else we'll make things hum for you."

Inspector Lamas then went to the door, feeling that it was up to him to do something for the credit he enjoyed. The previous week he had ordered a twenty-five-peso cake with the name Adela inscribed on it in green icing. Adela was one of his two mistresses, and the cake was for her birthday. Lamas had come right into the bakehouse and had specially requested that the cake be decorated with rose garlands. He still owed for the cake too.

He stood in the doorway and listened to the interchange. Then without a word he pulled out his revolver and with the butt end struck the picket who was standing nearest such a blow on the head that the blood spurted out. Then he whistled. Two policemen came up and he ordered them to conduct all the pickets and a few bystanders to the police station.

Just as they were marched off, Morales returned to the scene. He had been relieved for three hours and was just coming back to his post. When he heard what had happened, he shouted inside: "You son-of-a-bitch in there, now you'll be in for it. Just you see! We've only been playing so far, but we can change our tune." And away he went to the union office.

Within ten minutes the union Secretary arrived at the police station and demanded to see Inspector Lamas. "I want a few words with him. He must be drunk!"

The Inspector was summoned. When he arrived the Secretary then asked for the Police Superintendent, who came at once. He was quite disturbed when he saw the union Secretary, and he got right down to business.

"Why did you strike the picket?" the Superintendent asked Inspector Lamas.

"He was insulting people in the café."

The Superintendent looked at him, enraged. "What authority have you to strike a man who does nothing more than insult someone?"

Lamas was about to reply but the Superintendent cut him short. "Don't you know your regulations?" He turned to the clerk. "Record this: 'Lamas doesn't know his regulations'!"

Then he faced Lamas. "This isn't the right place for you, so I'll see about getting you transferred to a village where you can't make trouble. And if anything of the kind occurs again, the Police Department will have to dispense with your services. That won't be difficult. Now, why did you arrest these men?"

"They insulted all the guests and Señor Doux," Lamas said diffidently.

"Insulted? Insulted? What do you mean, insulted?"

"They called them sons-of-bitches."

"If you're going to arrest everyone who says son-of-a-bitch, you'll have to build a prison wall around the entire nation! You must be crazy."

"They threatened persons as well."

"Threatened? What do you mean by that?"

"They said they were going to kill Señor Doux."

"We said nothing of the kind!" the pickets called out.

The Superintendent looked scornfully at Lamas. "Hasn't anyone ever told you that he wanted to kill you? Your wife? Your friends? Acquaintances? And did you strike them on the head with your revolver butt?"

"Well, in this case it appeared to be very serious."

"Serious? For whom? Has one man of those you arrested struck anybody, or robbed or wrecked Señor Doux's café? Obviously not, or you would have told me right off. Yes, the police are here to protect the property and person of Señor Doux, but that isn't to say that we're here to back him up in paying wages on which no decent man can live, or to help him keep his men at work for such long hours that they haven't time even to take a promenade with their families. If the men put up with it, that's no affair of ours; but if they decide that they can't stand it any longer, then it's certainly no part of our duty to arrest them for that. Why can't Señor Doux come to terms with his men? If he did, he'd be left in peace. As it is, this disorder can't be allowed to continue, for it might lead to a serious breach of the peace. So I'm going to order the Café Aurora closed for two months; then we'll have some peace."

He turned to the clerk. "Draw up the closing order for two months, and I'll sign it now. And you, Señor Lamas, may consider yourself relieved of your office until I have the Governor's instructions for your station of transfer. The prisoners are released. Are there any other complaints?"

"No," answered the pickets.

The Superintendent got up and shook hands with the union Secretary, who was about to leave.

"The police of this district are no longer concerned with this affair," said the Superintendent. "Further developments are up to you. It was a good thing that I was called in so quickly, for there are always officers who are backward about these things."

"Backward, or don't want to keep up with the times because they have so many private obligations," the Secretary added.

"Lamas will get a district where he won't have expenses of that kind. I've already got a place in mind for him, a sort of bandit district. If he's got anything in him, he can show it there; and if he hasn't, we'll fire him. He's from the old school that thinks dictatorship is the best form of government. We'll soon have all the old ones out of our departments, and in the meantime, it's not a bad thing if the last of them give themselves away by slipping into their old habits."

"In other countries," exclaimed the Secretary, "for example in the United States, some of those reactionary old habits are ultramodern institutions."

"I know," answered the Superintendent. "We copy our neighbors in many things, but we mustn't copy them in everything, and we must be particularly careful not to copy those things that are out of keeping with the spirit of our times. The rough tactics are outdated and unjust. When it comes to asses of the two-legged species, the States have more than we have."

13

　　　Two police officials in green-braided uniforms called on Señor Doux and handed him the closing order. It came as a terrible shock to him, and he shouted to his wife: "Now, you see, we've got a proper Bolshevik government. They've played a nice trick on me."

"What's the matter?" she called as she came waddling up to him.

"They've closed us down."

"I always told you we shouldn't have come here. This country is stark, raving mad. There's no law and order here. You can go on paying your taxes, and paying them on the dot, but you never get a say in anything."

"You must close at once," said the official who had handed Doux the order, "or there will be a fine of over a hundred pesos."

"But surely my guests may finish their drinks?"

The official consulted his watch and said: "Half an hour, and then you must close. An officer will be posted here to see that no more customers are admitted. And you must pay the officer."

"*I* pay him?"

"You don't imagine that we'll pay him, do you? We have no funds available just to ensure that you obey the order."

The two officials went out, posted themselves at the entrance, and waited for the half hour of grace. When it was up, they shouted inside. Doux, furious with rage, shut the doors. Only the corridor entrance to the hotel remained open, for the hotel hadn't disturbed the peace.

Peace, however, didn't descend upon the café. On the contrary. Things became even livelier, for the Douxs themselves came to blows.

The Señora was consumed with fury; every centavo lost to the business ate into her heart. She waddled about in her slippers among the empty tables and made her husband's life a hell. She wore only a sleeveless negligee gathered loosely about her, the fat, flabby flesh of her bosom exposed, and bright yellow silk stockings over her bulging calves. Only her youth kept these overflowing masses looking somewhat more seductive than repulsive. Another five years and the seductiveness would certainly have vanished, leaving repulsiveness triumphant. The whole length of her arms protruded from the negligee, arms which might have passed for a wrestler's except that they were as flabby as the rest of her body. At the back of her neck there was a bulge of flesh that, for the present, protruded only shyly; but in a few years' time it would be a real landmark.

She always wandered about the place like this. Anywhere else she would have been taken for a brothel madame with whom it did not do to trifle. Occasionally she changed her negligee; she had a gray one, a pink one, a green one, a deep-yellow one, and a pale-mauve one. Whether or not she had other clothes I don't know, for I never saw her in anything else.

Señor Doux was always to be seen in shirt and trousers, and only when he went to the market did he put on a hat. He wore black trousers only, secured with a narrow leather belt, and a white shirt with a black bow tie. His belly stuck out in front of him like a balloon. The Señora too had a protruding paunch, but it was hidden in part by the loose negligee. Alas, what she had too much of in front she lacked behind. That isn't to say that there wasn't plenty behind, but the proportions in relation to her stomach were not generous enough to give her whole figure a harmony. All in all Doux could hardly complain, for he had in her something solid to hold on to, and was in no danger of chafing himself on protruding bones.

"You must have been off your head ever to have come to this crazy country," she was yelling at him.

"Me? Wasn't it you who kept telling me every day that millions were lying on the streets waiting to be shovelled up?"

"You dirty liar, you!" she howled. "You filthy Marseilles pimp! Didn't you draw out all my money and tell me that it'd earn a thousand percent in two years?"

"Well, wasn't I right? We came here with nothing—or how much was it? Eight hundred pesos? And I've already been offered sixty-eight thousand for the house and café. And why don't I sell? Because I know it's worth much more."

"Worth more?" she blazed. "Why, it's not worth a handful of horse shit! How can it be worth anything when it's closed? No one would give you the price of the bricks in it. And I told you that when the new government came in, that—what's-his-name?—that pig, one-armed general, that Obregon—yes, that's his name! He finished us off for good."

"How could I know this Revolution would change everything, even the value of the money, labor conditions, laws that affect property and all and everything that goes with it? But it's only since the new government that we've really begun to get anywhere. You wouldn't say that it was before then, eh?— when we had to grease everybody's palm with one hundred pesos, one after the other, for permission to breathe, even. Everybody was holding out a hand then."

"And now," she fired back at him, "is it any different? Now it's the working people who are holding out their hands. First in the kitchen, then the waiters, and you'll see, next will be the bakehouse. And when that comes, we might as well pack up and go home like beggars."

"Shut up, confound you!" he shrieked in full fury. "You spoil everything with your greed and your damned miserliness."

"Me, miserly? Miserly? If I didn't keep a hold on the money it would all go on you and your whores. And you call me miserly?"

Now we were hearing some fine family secrets. I could hardly believe the Señora was right; how could he have possibly found time for escapades? But of course their little dispute was really a conjugal dialogue, for they actually lived together in complete harmony which was disturbed only by the fact that the workers were waking up and taking an interest in their masters' profits. Similar displays of interest have been known to shake kings and to rock empires. So it wasn't surprising that the striking waiters gave the Douxs' domestic bliss a bit of a shaking.

The conjugal dialogues became not only more violent during the following days but also more frequent. They filled the days, and extended through the nights as the Douxs lay side by side in bed. We who were working there overheard the complete life history of each of them, from the day they were born to the moment when they came to blows with table lamp, wash basin, and chamber pot.

When they reached the stage where she was going around with the idea of putting rat poison into his coffee, and he was dreaming nightly of the razor with which he was going to slit her throat, he proved the superiority of man.

He went to the Superintendent of Police and asked what could be done to get the two months' closing order revoked and the waiters back into his café. The Superintendent told him that he himself could do nothing in this case. It was a matter of coming to terms with the union; the café couldn't be operated until the dispute between the two was settled.

"Then I'm bankrupt," said Doux. "And the waiters will be thrown out of work."

"Don't worry about them, señor," the Superintendent replied. "As long as people want to sit in a café and spoon up strawberry ice, they'll want waiters to serve them. You can see that from the Moderna, which is always full now. All your old customers go there, of course. But I can't do anything about it. Your premises are closed, and they'll stay closed for the two-month period. My advice is, go to the union and arrange things with them."

On the afternoon of the same day Doux met Morales, whom he approached with all humility.

"Listen, Morales," he said, "I'll agree to everything. Could you see to it that the waiters return to my place?"

Morales eyed him coolly from head to foot and said: "Do I know you? Oh, yes, you're Doux of La Aurora. But we waiters have nothing to do with you; we walked out remember? If you want anything with us, you must go to the union. Adios."

Doux wrote a letter to the union saying that he would like an interview with the Secretary; he ventured to ask the Secretary to call on him to discuss the situation of the waiters' strike.

On the following day he received his reply. It was just one sharp sentence: "If you want anything from the union, the address of the office is: Calle Madero No. 18, Second Floor. The Secretary hadn't even considered it necessary to sign his name.

For Señor Doux there was no alternative but to go, for the razor was haunting him day and night, so that even when he was eating he had the feeling that his table knife was a razor.

"Take a seat in the waiting room," said a worker in the union office. "There's a conference on, but it won't last long."

It lasted over half an hour, and while he was waiting Doux had time to digest the slogans displayed on the walls. Those slogans made him angry at first. But the longer he studied them, the more he came to fear what lay in store for him behind the Secretary's door, through which he could hear the tapping of a typewriter.

At last a worker appeared. "The Secretary will see you now, señor," he said.

Doux swallowed nervously as he stepped into the small room that was the Secretary's office. He had intended to look the Secretary straight in the eye, but he found that he couldn't; again, his gaze was drawn to the walls, for behind the Secretary's desk the entire wall was covered with a red and black flag, while above the flag in bold letters screamed the slogan: PROLETARIOS DEL MUNDO, UNIOS!

This put Doux quite off his stride. His voice, which he had wanted to sound firm and resolute, faltered timidly as he said: "Good day. I am Señor Doux of the Café Aurora."

"Right," said the Secretary. "Sit down. And what do you want?"

"I'd like to know if you can arrange for my café to be reopened."

"Yes, that can be arranged," the Secretary replied, "provided you fulfill certain conditions."

"Oh, I'm ready to agree to everything that the waiters are demanding."

The Secretary took up a sheet of paper, glanced at it, and said: "The waiters' demands are no longer the same as those put forward when they first spoke with you."

"Not the same?" gulped Doux, frightened.

"No, it's fifteen pesos a week now," said the Secretary in the manner of a businessman.

"But they were asking twelve."

"That may be. But then they went on strike. You don't suppose the men are going to strike for nothing, do you? Now it's fifteen. If you'd agreed at once it'd have been twelve."

"All right," said Doux, straightening up, "I agree to fifteen."

"Friday is pay day, for the whole week. Irregular or postponed pay days can no longer be permitted," continued the Secretary.

"But I can't pay just like that. It has been our practice to pay when we had available cash."

The Secretary looked up. "What always has been your practice is neither here nor there. We are deciding what you must do from now on. We are at last putting a stop to abuses that have gone on here for hundreds of years. There is the work, here are the wages. And you must pay the wages just as punctually as you expect the men to do their work."

"But that's going to be difficult," said Doux, defensively, "because if I pay out the wages like that I might find myself without sufficient cash to do the buying on Saturday."

"That's nothing to do with us. Wages must come first, or the workers will find themselves without sufficient cash to do *their* buying. And, in our view, it's better for you to be short of cash than the workers."

Doux was breathing heavily. "But the work week doesn't end until Saturday. Why should I pay the wages on Friday?"

"Why? Why? You mean you don't understand?" The Secretary affected surprise. "The worker gives you five days' credit. He gives you his output for five whole days while you do business with the capital of his labor. Why should the worker be called upon to lend you his five days' output? Actually, you should pay for the whole week in advance, on

Monday morning; that would be the proper thing to do. But we don't want to go that far."

"All right, then, I'll agree to that, too. And to one full meal and rolls and coffee at another hour. So then, everything's in order?" Doux got up.

"Sit down for a moment," invited the Secretary. "There are still one or two minor points to settle. You must pay for the strike days."

"Me? Pay for the strike days? Am I to pay for idleness too?"

"Striking is not idling," said the Secretary firmly, "and if your men go on strike, you must pay their full wages. Otherwise, all you hotel and café proprietors could force us into a long strike and so whittle away our funds that we could never strike again. Oh, no, señor, we're not having anything like that. The strike is financed by us. We act as a kind of loan office for the workers, but you are the one who must pay for the strike. You had ample time to make up your mind whether or not to let it come to a strike. The cost of war must be borne by the party who needs peace in order to get on with his business."

"This is the greatest injustice I've ever met," exclaimed Doux.

"Well, if you like, I'll enumerate the injustices that you and your kind have been perpetrating for years."

"Obviously, I have no alternative but to pay for it all," Doux admitted, dejectedly.

"And preferably today," declared the Secretary, "for tomorrow it will cost you another day."

"Then I'll come back here before five o'clock and settle the whole business," said Doux, and he got up for the second time.

"Bring a little extra with you," the Secretary advised as he also got to his feet.

"Still more?" exclaimed Doux.

"Yes, I thought you wanted the café reopened now, not in two months' time."

"Isn't that part of the bargain, if I agree to everything?" Doux was getting jumpy.

"By no means," answered the Secretary. "The closing of the café was for reasons apart from the waiters' strike. You know that as well as I do. You asked Inspector Lamas to give the pickets a beating."

"I certainly did not!" insisted Doux.

"Obviously we don't agree on that. In any case, it happened on your premises and so you must be held responsible for it. You might easily have prevented it."

"Come on, then, tell me what else I've got to do," urged Doux.

"You must pay ten thousand pesos into the funds of our union as compensation. As soon as you've paid it, we shall take over the guarantee to the Governor on your behalf. And then the café can be reopened."

"Am I expected to pay ten thousand pesos?" Doux dropped into the chair again, breaking out in a cold sweat.

"You need not pay it; we're not forcing you. But then the café will stay closed for two months," the Secretary continued matter-of-factly. "And of course at the end of the two months you would have to pay the waiters retroactively. They must live. And we can't allow them to take on any other work, since they must be ready to go to work for you as soon as you reopen your café. It would be too bad if you had no waiters on your reopening day.

"To make the situation clear to you, once and for all: It isn't our intention to destroy business or even interfere with it, certainly not. It is, however, our intention and purpose to see to it that the worker gets not only a fair share of what he produces, but the share which is due him up to the maximum that the business can afford. And this maximum is much higher than you imagine. At present we're conducting a thorough inquiry into the capacity of every branch of industry, and those branches which can't bring a decent living wage to the worker must go to the wall. And we'll see to it that they do. If such industries are important to the community, then we'll see to it that the community guarantees the worker a decent living standard. For example, I wouldn't swear to it that your café is indispensable to the community; but it's there. And as long as you operate it to increase your own fortune, it must bring in enough to pay decent wages to the workers there. If the time comes when you can't make a profit from it, you'll close it down of your own accord.

"Well, Señor Doux, I've told you all this so that you won't think we're just a bunch of blackmailers. No, all we want is that the men who are making a fortune for you receive the share to which they're entitled; and there'll still be enough left over for you."

Doux had only half understood what the Secretary was saying. He sat there, dazed. His head swam with the thought of laying out ten thousand pesos. He didn't dare say yes for fear of his señora, for he didn't know what she'd prefer to do. Every day's delay cost money. Yet, it would cost him more than the ten thousand pesos if the business had to remain closed for two months, with back pay on top of that. He kept juggling the figures in his head until he thought he'd go mad.

At last he got up. "I'll think it over," he said.

He left the office, went down the stairs, and stepped out into the street. He wiped the sweat from his face and gasped for air. Then he started walking home. The walk cooled him down, so that he calmly began to consider the matter. He sat on a park bench to make various calculations on a piece of paper and eventually reached the conclusion that it would be cheaper to pay up everything at once. But what about Señora Doux? If he went home first, there would be a scrap. If he said yes outright, she'd say, "Why don't you say no?" And if he said no, she'd say, "Why don't you say yes?"

Whatever he did would be wrong, for it would cost money, and a great deal of money; and anything that cost money and didn't bring in double always caused a row with the Señora. At last, however, Doux was seized by a proud and manly courage which urged him, for once, to enforce his own independent will without consulting his wife. And he thought that he could best do this by shouldering the decision that was most likely to throw her into a rage: to go to the bank, draw out all the necessary money, and, without a word to his wife, go to the union office and settle everything without further ado.

Half an hour later he had paid up every peso that was demanded.

"You may reopen your café at seven this evening," said the Secretary. "I'll see to it that the revocation order is in your hands by that time."

Doux folded the receipts, each one duly affixed with the legal stamps. "Señor Secretary, there's one small point I'd like to make."

"Well?"

"Must I really pay the wages for the whole week on Fridays?"

"You had better, Señor Doux."

"What happens then if a man is paid on Friday and doesn't show up on Saturday? He'd have rooked me out of a whole day's pay."

"My, my," said the Secretary, smiling, "but you're good at figures. I'd never have expected it of you. You've held back the men's wages for as much as six weeks, not one day, remember, but six weeks."

"But the men always got their wages in the long run. They knew they were safe, anyhow," and Doux puffed out his chest.

"Whether you're as solid as all that is still very much open to question. You could sell out secretly and make off with the wages due; some employers have done that. But that probably wouldn't happen in your case. What has happened is that you've always held onto the wages for a few weeks and made use of money that belonged to the waiters without paying them any interest. Why should the workers be expected to lend you their wages free of charge? This must stop. You can count yourself very lucky that we haven't required the whole week's wages to be paid on Wednesdays, so that the risk would be equally divided. We'll leave it at Friday. If you treat the men decently, none of them will run off with that one day's pay. But if a worker should do it once in a while it won't ruin you. Well, that answers your question. You'd better run along now, so that you can be ready for your customers at seven o'clock."

Doux left the office and made his way home.

14

 "That's quite sensible, what you've done," said Señora Doux, to Doux's complete surprise. "But if things had been done my way in the first place, we could have saved ourselves all this trouble."

"Your way?" asked Señor Doux. "Everything was always done your way. It was you who were always telling me to fire the waiters, that waiters were two for a penny, anyway."

"Well, that was true, wasn't it? They were falling over themselves to get work, then. I never thought there'd come a day when all we could get would be two tramps. That was where my calculations went wrong. Don't worry, we'll soon recover the money. The bakery and pastry shop will have to make up for it. They're a better lot of workers than the waiters; at least they're not bolshies."

So there it was. We in the bakery and pastry shop had to make good the loss. Now Doux invested in publicity. Ads in newspapers and movie houses declared the excellence of his bread, his cakes, and his pastries.

The result of this was that we now had to start work at ten every night, Saturdays at nine, and work through until four, sometimes five o'clock the next afternoon. That became a new rule. If anyone didn't like it, he left; and Doux would then declare that no one had applied for the job, and that the rest of us would have to take over the man's work for the time being. Sometimes it happened that two men quit on the same day, and then there was the work of two men to make up for.

Doux would put off replacing the missing workers as long as possible so as to save the wages. We knew this because we sent men to him and he told them there was no vacancy. This went on until we simply left orders unfilled. When it was a case of an order for a birthday cake or some other food for a special occasion, it went badly for Señora Doux. Of course the Señor would make himself scarce and she would have to fight it out with the customer. At last this got to be too much for her, so she herself would hire one or two new men, always the cheapest she could get, men who knew nothing about the trade and hadn't the intelligence to pick it up quickly.

The master baker had daily arguments with Doux over supplies. One day the sugar supply was very low. The master went to Doux and told him that we needed two hundred kilos of sugar.

"All right, all right," said Doux, "I'll order some right away."

But he put off ordering it, just to keep the money in his pocket a few days longer. The moment came when we had no sugar at all, and we were having rows with the waiters who came into the bakehouse to take the last scrapings from the barrel for the café, where every sugar bowl was empty. Then Doux rushed off in a frenzy to get the sugar in as quickly as he could, while we in the bakehouse had to stand about and wait, as we couldn't bake without sugar; worse, we couldn't clean up and go to bed, for the baked goods had to be finished.

It was the same with the eggs. Five hundred cases were ordered one week, and they were delivered. Then, when we were working on the last fifty cases, the master told Doux that it was time to order more eggs.

"Can't it wait until tomorrow?" asked Doux.

"Yes, it can wait until tomorrow, but not a moment longer."

"That's all right, then," said Doux, mightily pleased that he could put it off for one day.

Next morning the master had to run to him again. "It's getting urgent. By day after tomorrow we'll be all out of eggs."

This time Doux didn't ask if it could wait until the next day; but he put it off, on his own responsibility. And so the moment came when we were all standing about, just waiting for eggs.

And it was the same story with the ice. The ice cream had to be ready by two o'clock. We might have the mixture ready in good time, but the ice wouldn't be on hand because Doux had ordered it too late. It would arrive at three or four, when it should have arrived at one o'clock, and so we would have to stand around two or three hours, unable to knock off work until the ice cream was ready for the café.

That was how we wasted our time, not working time, but our own free time, just because Doux wanted to hang on to his money for a few more hours; and because our time was bought by him not by the hour but by the day. Each minute of our lives belonged to him; he bought it and paid for it, by way of our meager wages.

If we didn't like it, well, it was true that we could leave. We could go and starve, for jobs were few and far between; and any available work was snapped up by local men who did it for a wage on which it was impossible to live—even if you did see them and their families living on it.

There wasn't any choice. You either had to starve or do as the boss wanted. He couldn't do as he liked with the waiters anymore, so we had to cope with everything that he couldn't push onto them. We were the rabble. If we quit, there were twenty more waiting outside only too pleased to get into a bakery where there was not only plenty of bread and cake to eat, but where there were even regular meals, the like of which these hungry men had never seen on their own tables.

The waiters were intelligent fellows, Mexicans and Spaniards, alert and active. But we in the bakery were gathered in from the road and the bush, without family or fixed abode. Some couldn't even speak Spanish. Our working conditions and wages didn't offer the slightest inducement to workers with any pride. We had a certain individualistic common pride, but you can't reform the living conditions of the worker with that; for the employer has pride enough of that kind himself and he knows how to use it to his own advantage. That battlefield is his; he knows every trick and can parry every thrust with success. We itinerant workers were simply attempting to save a little money and start a small business, or scrape together the fare for a try somewhere else—Colombia or wherever. We were trying to get as much from the furrow we were plowing as we possibly could. Whether those who came after us fell by the wayside was a matter of indifference to us. Everyone is his own best friend. If the grass gets scarce while I'm grazing I'll pull up the roots as well.

Doux and the other businessmen in town knew how to keep us too busy at work to learn to think for ourselves. It was a new country, as far as business ventures went. Everybody had but one thought and that was to get rich, and to get rich quick, without regard to what happened to the other fellow. That was the way of the oil people, the mining people, the merchants, hotel proprietors, plantation owners—in fact of anyone who had a few pesos. They must all exploit something or someone. If they couldn't exploit an oil field or a silver mine, or customers or hotel guests, they would exploit the hunger of the down-and-outers. Everyone must bring in money, and everything did bring in money. There was gold in the veins and muscles of the hungry workers as surely as there was gold in the gold mines. To exploit a gold mine a great deal of capital was needed and risked. To exploit an oil field might mean drilling ten times to a depth of two thousand five hundred feet, at great expense, to get nothing but dry holes in the end. But as long as any worker could move his limbs he was no dry hole; he was more conveniently exploited than any gold mine or oil field.

Take Apfel, a Hungarian. He arrived in Mexico with a few hundred pesos in his pocket but couldn't find work. So he rented a small shack and bought tools from one junk dealer and some old sheet iron from another; out of this junk he made buckets and water tanks.

One day a man came and said: "Could you make me a tank?"

"Sure, if you give me an advance of one hundred pesos," said Apfel.

But he couldn't make this tank single-handed.

In a Chinese eating joint he ran into a compatriot from Budapest, begging and in rags. The man had come into the joint, gone up to Apfel's table, and asked in broken Spanish if he might have the half of a roll which was lying there unwanted.

"Take it," said Apfel. "Aren't you Hungarian?"

"Yes, I'm from Budapest."

So they conversed in Hungarian.

"Are you looking for work?" Apfel asked.

"Yes, I've been looking for work for a long while, but there's nothing."

"No, there's not much of anything," Apfel agreed, "but I can get you work."

"Really? I'd be so grateful if you could."

"But it means a fourteen-hour stretch."

"That's all right, as long as it's work and pays money for food."

"The pay's not so good either. Only about two pesos and fifty centavos."

"I'd be satisfied with that."

"Then come tomorrow morning," said Apfel, and he explained how to find his work shack. "I work there, too; I've got a small contract."

"I'm glad to be working with a fellow countryman."

"You may well be," said Apfel, "for who else would take you on? There's absolutely no work to be had."

The man started to work for Apfel, and he worked with a will. Fourteen hours a day. In a tropical country. In a wooden shack under a corrugated iron roof. Two pesos fifty a day. Fifty centavos a night for a bed—no, not quite a bed, but a wooden frame with a piece of canvas stretched across it. In a flophouse, where bugs and mosquitoes made each night a hell. Fifty centavos for a noon comida at the Chink's, and fifty more for a supper there. Twenty centavos for a cup of breakfast coffee and ten centavos for two dry rolls. A few cigarettes a day. A glass of ice water for five centavos—perhaps two or three glasses during the long day. Then his shirt fell to pieces, his shoes already having gone west before he began to work for Apfel. New shoes consumed a full week's work, a shirt two days' work, always assuming that he bought nothing to eat. This went on for two weeks, three weeks, four weeks. Then he was taken to the local poorhouse—malaria, fever, God knows what. Two days later he was crammed into a pine box and shoved into the ground.

But Apfel fulfilled his contract for the tank and got an order for three more of the same. He could always find more starving immigrants, if not Hungarians, then Austrians, or Germans, or Poles, or Czechs. The port was swarming with them; and they were all so grateful to Apfel for giving them work. Now it was only a twelve-hour day; he moved ahead with the times and didn't want to exploit the unemployed. But it was still two-fifty a day, with three-fifty for the foreman whom he now needed. It was going on four years since he had made his first tank; and he was driving his own car and had built a house for himself in the North American Quarter.

Yes, even the bones of a compatriot to whom you extended a helping hand and who, because of this help, because of overwork, because of the rat hole in which he slept, because of the lack of proper nourishment died of fever and was buried in a pauper's grave—even this could be turned into gold.

The Budapest newspapers reported that citizen Apfel had, "by his industry and enterprise made a sizable fortune in a few years." Fortunes were made overnight that way. All you had to do was to exploit the various kinds of gold mines.

And the foreigners could do it more handily than anyone else, for if natives and noncompatriots made trouble for them, they claimed the protection of their embassy; and then freedom-loving America would threaten military intervention.

15

The dormitory for the bakery help was a huge wooden box with a tin roof—you couldn't have called it a house. Daylight entered through window openings which were innocent of either glass or screen. Six wooden steps led up to the door; the space underneath them was crammed with old egg crates, empty cans, old rope, and rotten rags, and there were packs of rats running wild among the junk. During the rainy season this became a swamp hole and an ideal breeding ground for hundreds of thousands of mosquitoes.

The dormitory room, just big enough to permit passage between the contraptions that we called our beds, served not only as our home but also as the home of great lizards, huge cockroaches, and spiders. There were also three dogs wandering about our place; one of them had mange and was horrible to look at. When he got better, the others got it. But the dogs were very fond of us and we didn't chase them away; they were our only solace on those days when we had no time or strength to take a walk in the streets or the park and fell into our canvas cots, too worn out to sleep.

Occasionally Antonio or I would sweep the room. It was

never scrubbed, but, as the roof leaked, we got plenty of water inside whenever there was a tropical downpour, which during the last weeks of the rainy season happened every half hour. We got bathed in bed, too, and our night's rest was a game of getting up during rainstorms, again and again, to push our beds under some section of the roof where we imagined no rain would trickle through.

Each of us had a mosquito net, or bar, as they are called. But they were full of holes, and the mosquitoes not only found the tears with the greatest of ease but also came through those places which we imagined were free of holes. We sewed up the nets as best we could, but on the following day a rip would start from the old hole. You could say that each net consisted of a number of large holes held together by shreds of rotten fabric.

In addition to this net we each had a tattered blanket and a dirty pillow. On the wall our predecessors had left us an old mirror in a tin frame, a few photos of nude girls, and some other photographs of the kind which, in many countries, would come within the province of the public prosecutor. No fine arts commission, however progressive, could possibly have defended these photographs, for they had absolutely nothing to do with art and had everything to do with nature's processes. But in a country where a boy of ten can buy them as easily as a gray-haired sailor, they are of no special interest; it's always only the forbidden fruit that tempts. So we saw nothing special about the photos. We didn't have time to bother about them.

Between nine and two in the daytime you couldn't stay in the dormitory; if you'd tried you'd have turned into seared meat. But of course we didn't try, because during those hours we were working in front of the bakery ovens. And just at the time of night when it began to get cool and we could have enjoyed a gorgeous sleep, we had to get out and go to work.

The work itself wasn't hard; I couldn't say that it was. But being on your feet for eighteen hours or so without a break, constantly running to and fro, bending down and reaching up, putting things here and carrying them there tires you out far more than working hard for eight hours in one spot. It was always "Quick, quick, the round rolls out of the oven. . . . Hurry up, the devil take you, get those trays greased. . . . Damn you, fix the beater into the mixer. . . . Quick, quick, I gotta have the egg whites beaten. . . . That mixture's too salty; hurry, hurry, take it away and mix one up again. . . . I want two kilos of icing, I told you that an hour ago. . . . Why, damn it, why didn't you boil up the caramel yesterday? Now we're sunk. . . . Holy smoke, now José has to slip up with the ice cream mix, and the slop's all over the floor. Thanks a lot, José, we'll all be here until six again today, if that's the way you're doing things." There was a constant hustle and bustle and bullying and scurrying. I'm sure that I covered a good twenty miles a day, rushing up and down that bakehouse.

Then there was the constant change of staff. Hardly had a new man been trained than another left. In fact, training the men was our biggest stumbling block. Doux would say: "Now you've got two new men whom I've got to pay, and yet you're not getting any more stuff baked. What's the point of my hiring new men? There's nothing to show for it."

In a sense he was right, but that was because no new hands knew anything about baking. They had to be shown everything, even how to handle a hot baking tray or a wooden spoon; and while you were showing them you could have done it yourself ten times over. A few picked it up quickly, but most would get under our feet and only succeed in slowing us down. We had one pastry cook who couldn't manage the simplest flaky pastry although he could produce recommendations from first-class patisseries.

It was the aliens who made the money for Doux. They were the ones he could exploit to the limit. The Mexican workers would put up with things for two, three, or maybe four weeks; then they'd say, "There's too much work here!" and they'd quit. By then they had perhaps saved a few pesos to start up a small business in cigarettes, chewing gum, leather belts, revolver holsters, candy, fruit—things of that kind. Their trade would bring them a profit of about one peso a day, but they managed on it and they remained free men. Some of these small traders climbed higher and higher until they could rent some small, dark alcove—what you might call a hole in the wall—in a narrow street, where they set up shop. But we stayed on, being afraid to lose that security the bakery offered us.

Of course, we wouldn't have been content with one peso of daily profit, for we made much more, one twenty-five with room and board. And we wanted more out of life. Those who worked just long enough to save a little money to make themselves independent were content with cotton pants at three pesos fifty a pair; but such pants weren't good enough for us. Ours had to cost seven or eight pesos. We felt that if we allowed ourselves to be seen in anything less expensive we would lose our dignity and status as white men. The "free" men bought shoes for six or eight pesos a pair. We wouldn't have dared to cross the street in such footwear. Think what we'd look like! We simply couldn't do it, if only on account of the señoritas. So our shoes never cost less than sixteen or eighteen pesos. After all, we were white men; and in order to remain so in the eyes of the other whites—Americans, British, Spaniards, French, and so on—we had to remain slaves to the bakehouse, earning good wages. Noblesse oblige—all the more so in tropical countries where the whites are only a small minority in the overwhelmingly native population.

It should be admitted however that, although we made the

greatest efforts not to lose caste, we lived in an uncertain social position. The Americans, British, and Spaniards did not consider us their equals. To them we were still only filthy scum, the scum that sticks to the heels of the prosperous whites and follows them about the world, and this we remained. But it is the big bosses, the power-hungry and the profit-hunters, who create the scum; then, when conditions become too hot and they are called upon to clean it up, they just pack up their profits, go home, and let the scum rot.

We did not even belong to the mixed-bloods, the Mestizos, to whom we were alien rabble. Nor were we accepted by the pure-blooded natives, the tribes or subnations of Indians all over the Republic. They would have little to do with metropolitan migrant workers, half-vagabonds such as we. Although every native and at least two-thirds of the Mestizos were proletarian like us, we were nevertheless separated from them by a gulf that couldn't be bridged. Language, past, habits, customs, philosophies, views, and ideas were so utterly different that no common link could be forged.

One pay day Antonio and I decided to go shopping. He bought a new hat, shirt, and shoes. I treated myself to a new pair of pants and a pair of smart brown shoes, which to make them appear as having been imported from England were called Oxfords, and so stamped in big letters on the soles. Naturally, that word alone, not the quality of the material or the manufacture, explained the extra high price I had to pay for them.

We went straight back to the dormitory and got into our new clothes.

"What'll we do with the money we've got left?" said Antonio.

"That's what I'd like to know," I said. "I've been thinking there's no use in collecting a lot of stuff we don't want."

"No, no point at all," confirmed Antonio.

"But it'd be silly to keep the money in our pockets," I went on.

"Yes," agreed Antonio, "it would be silly, for it might be stolen."

"And I don't think it's a good idea to put it in the bank, either," I declared.

"We'd only be making ourselves ridiculous if we took our few pesos in and asked to open a bank account," said Antonio, and he was right.

"We'd never live it down," I said. "Anyhow, the bank's closed now, and we can't get there when it's open because those are the hours when we're working."

"What'll we do with the money then? I've absolutely no desire for tequila now," Antonio confessed.

"Me neither. I can't stand the smell of it right now."

"You know what we could do?" ventured Antonio.

"Well?"

"We could go down to see the señoritas."

"Great idea, Antonio! At least we'd know where and for what our money was blown, and, after all, we couldn't put it to better use!"

"Sure, Gales, you're right there. We'll go nuts if all we do is work in the bakehouse and sleep in that rat hole."

"Yes, and those photos on the wall are getting pretty dull, Antonio. I can't stand the sight of those stupid paper girls much longer."

"Neither can I. It's almost as if we're married to them. They seem to follow us with their eyes and watch everything we do. I'm fed up with them. We need some new faces!"

With this, Antonio got up from the edge of his cot, went over to the wall, and tore down all the beautiful naked women. Then each of us put aside one silver peso which we hid in an old shoe; we agreed that we'd buy new women and new photos of lively doings and inspiring positions to adorn our lonely walls and thus save our fancies from starvation.

Then, so as to be able to make the right impression on the señoritas, we spruced ourselves up and went in search of the real thing, warmer and sweeter than mere pictures, where life was not harsh but beautiful.

It was already evening. We had a fairly long way to go, because the señoritas lived on the outskirts of town where they had a whole quarter to themselves. This was as agreeable to them as to the men who wanted to enjoy the good things of life without having to shoulder any obligations in return.

16

  We were greeted by the sound of music and gay laughter; with every step that brought us nearer to the girls the drabness and monotony of life receded. Beauty prevails where music and laughter are.

Along the houses of the quarter were concrete sidewalks, barely two feet wide. The street lay three feet and often more below the level of the sidewalk; there being no steps, you jumped if you wanted to get down. The streets were muddy, smelly swamps; stones and chunks of broken concrete lying about and deep holes filled with water left over from the last heavy rain made them practically impassable. Nevertheless, cars and taxis churned their way through to bring, wait for, and pick up passengers. Frequently, cars got stuck in the mud and then there was a great clattering, banging, and hollering as they worked their way out. The drivers didn't complain, but laughed and took it as part of the game, without which the quarter most certainly wouldn't have been what it was.

At street corners were small groups of strolling musicians who played very well, much better in fact than the street bands in town, where there were so many that they stumbled over each other's feet. The bands usually consisted of a violin, cello, clarinet, flute, and drum. Some had a trumpet instead of a flute. Others had a violin, saxophone, cello, and guitar, and these were invariably the best. After they performed they passed a hat around, but it was rare for a visitor to put in something, and it was mostly the girls who gave them money.

The bands also went into the restaurants and bars and played there, where their chances of money, if slim, were better than out in the street. In every café and bar there was dancing, for every place had its girls who were supposed to smile and dance and drink with the customers, and whose chief job it was to make them spend money, of which they of course got their percentage.

While they were dancing the little people could tell each other everything that was uppermost in their hearts without saying a word. There were no taboos as to the style or manner of dancing. Consequently, most people danced so decently that the angels in heaven could have watched without blushing. But now and then a couple might dance in a style that would have made the devil's grandmother hide her face in her apron. But she did not see it, having more dire things to watch elsewhere, and other people did not worry about it; and the patroling policeman lit a cigarette, watched smiling for a second, and continued on his beat.

A Negro dancer from Virginia was performing in La Casa Roja as we were passing. She was alone in the center of the café, dancing the belly dance—but the genuine belly dance, the belly dance that Eve invented after she got out of Paradise and could do as she pleased. Not only the men but all the girls in the place rose to watch this piece of supreme art, and perhaps to learn gestures and rhythms that might be useful to them when they weren't sleeping alone. Those out in the street pushed in at the open doors to look on.

At the end of the dance, she sank to the floor. Deafening

applause rang out from every side. There she knelt, her arms thrown back, her breasts quivering, her body rippling and heaving with a final expiring sigh such as might follow the last tired drop of a dying mountain stream. Wearily she drew in her belly and let her head drop, tired and spent, until her forehead touched the floor. Then she sprang up with a jubilant cry of deep and healthy joy; slim and erect she stood there, her left hand pressed against her hip, her right thrown high in a gently rounded gesture. Her eyes sparkled and her white teeth gleamed between her full lips. And she laughed a victorious laugh, arched her body forward with an eagerness which seemed to invite a whole continent to embrace her, and cried out, "Viva el amor y la alegria, amigos! Viva el amor! Viva!"

A short silence followed. Then the applause thundered out again, the music following it loudly. Now the dancer tugged her thin gown into place, smoothed back her thick hair, and stepped to her table where only her bottle and a glass awaited her.

What is art? Art is that which amazes and rejoices our souls. Thus, the belly dance of the Virginia Negress was true art, natural and mature.

The men were looking at her with awe and genuine admiration but, strangely enough, none approached her or asked her to dance. Perhaps, because she was an artist, favored by the gods, they felt they did not have enough to offer her. They went up to other girls who were more modest in appearance and who didn't give intimations of such hurricanes of passion as would threaten to unhorse the most accomplished Casanova.

The girls didn't regard the dancer as a rival competing by unfair means—not in the least; for she gave the business an élan which it had lacked ten minutes earlier. Now the men had fire in their eyes, whereas before they had appeared indifferent, disinterested—yes, even bored.

Antonio and I had been watching from the doorway of the café, and I had lost him in the crowd. Now I saw him inside. He had found himself a dancing partner. So I left him at the Casa Roja and went out to have a look around the quarter.

The streets were crowded with vendors, their tiny temporary stalls giving the whole place the atmosphere of a fair. There were stalls that served hot enchiladas, stalls offering tacos, crisp rolls filled with roast beef, ham, fried fish, sausage, or cheese. There were hot tamales and corn on the cob for sale. You could buy avocados, bananas, oranges, slices of watermelon and pineapple, and chunks of coconut. Some small booths sold cigarettes, cigars, pipe tobacco, candy, newspapers, and magazines—local ones and foreign (American, British, French, or what have you). At many little table stalls you could buy iced drinks in half a dozen exotic flavors—horchata, jamaica, tamarindo, chia, papaya, and mamey. And in the thick of the swarming streets women and boys approached the crowds carrying baskets or cigar boxes filled with candy, chewing gum, matches, lottery tickets, toasted pumpkin seeds, peanuts, sugar-coated fruits, and flowers.

More than a hundred traders made their living here. Women nursed their babies in their arms and led their small children by the hand as they sold their goods. Neither the morals of the teenagers who shouted their wares for sale nor those of the women vendors and the children at their skirts were endangered in this environment.

Hundreds of respectable women, girls, and children—whole families, in fact—passed through the quarter to reach their homes. They thought nothing of it. To the pure, all things are pure. They could have gone another way, but the way through the quarter was the most direct.

In the whole section only four policemen and an officer were needed. They seldom had trouble to straighten out; and if they did, it was regarded as an event. Very few drunks had to be taken into custody, for drunks were rarely seen there. Besides the uniformed police, there were two or three plain-clothesmen, who mingled with the people, on the lookout for international opium, marijuana, and cocaine dealers who might be doing business in the area.

The other representatives of the authorities in power that you could see snaking their way through the crowd were the inspectors of the Public Health Department and, of course, the tax collectors. Everybody around here, itinerant trader, stall owner, or barkeeper, and of course the ever-smiling girls, had to pay taxes; not by next April, oh no, but right here and on the spot, in cash, no checks accepted—or out you go immediately. The taxes, high or low, were paid not just because the tax collector was such a pleasant fellow; taxpayers got an unlimited protection for their business. And as you would expect in a really democratic Republic, in any doubtful case the girls got an immediate and a better protection than the men who tried to run away without paying for the services they had received.

The girls who were at the top of their profession spoke not only French, but also English, German, and Italian, in addition to Spanish; for certain forms of entertainment are more pleasurable when accompanied by the music of the mother tongue, and certain sensations come to full flowering when aroused by .'ords that strike chords and memories which a strange language never can touch. Such words bring back the memory of the first feeling of shame, thoughts of the first girl you desired, and sensations of those mysterious hours which ushered in the first feeling of maturity.

Therefore most of the poor girls with only Spanish at their command didn't get on well, and were soon taking in the one-peso trade—native workers, poor devils, who couldn't afford to lay out much cash on recreation of this kind. These girls lived in remote parts of the quarter, where the rooms, or cribs, were the cheapest and most crudely furnished and where street musicians strayed only occasionally, that is, when the competition was too strong elsewhere. In this area, the girls dressed so simply that they could go to town without attracting attention. Their earnings at times were barely sufficient to buy rouge and powder, yet they had to have water, soap, antiseptic solution, and clean towels for every visitor. At any time an Inspector of the Sanitary Commission might enter the room, demand a look at the girl's health certificate, and inspect the room for cleanliness. The girls' personal effects were their own affairs, but the other standard items had to conform with health regulations, or else there would be quarantine, which was a costly business, more to be dreaded than a fine or a jail sentence.

Yet, there was no slavery. Every girl was a free agent. She could leave the house and the quarter at any moment she chose. There was no old madame who could detain her under some pretext of a rent pledge, unearned board, or a laundry bill. Rent had to be paid one week in advance, and that was that; if she couldn't pay in advance she had to leave the quarter. Any girl caught soliciting in the streets was put into jail.

In the so-called Golden Section at the entrance to the quarter, flooded by the brilliant lights of the dance halls, lived the French girls. They spoke a torrentially rapid French, and all of them swore that they were Parisiennes; most of them, of course, never had set eyes on Paris, but came from London, Berlin, Naples, Budapest, Warsaw, Leningrad, and places even farther from the French capital. None of them had official passports, for ladies devoting themselves to this most ancient profession are not permitted to immigrate; but they got in, somehow, each one by a different trick.

The Parisiennes were the most elegant girls in the quarter; they had to be, to keep going in the Golden Section. The moment their earnings ceased to afford the necessary trappings, a thing that could happen quickly and did happen often, the girls had to move to the next cheaper section. And so it would come to pass with many a girl who didn't sufficiently understand the business, and failed to learn the tricks which might have made her the mistress of her trade, that she had to move farther and farther away from the Golden Section until she ended up in the cribs in the lowliest area of all.

The girls in the Golden Section were visited by men to whom dollars and pesos were as nothing, such as the oilmen who had lived in the bush for six or eight months where they couldn't spend money, and who came with thousands of dollars burning holes in their pockets. Perhaps they would start out intending to spend no more than twenty, yet might end up next morning begging a peso to get back to the hotel by second-class bus. Then there were those American tourists who came to the country for no other pleasure but just this one, and of course overpaid for every service. There were also the speculators who sold shares of oil stock, gold or silver mines to greenhorns, shares in phantom wells in areas where no oil would be found unless the poor investor carried a can of it to the place. These men, loaded with cash so easily acquired, went from house to house and girl to girl with inexhaustible vitality. Mind you, they went to the mistresses of the art, those highly experienced females who could have made a lively fountain spurt from the driest tree trunk.

The houses of the quarter were mainly of wood and they all looked alike, lined up side by side like Baltimore row houses. They were with few exceptions one-room affairs; the room had only one door which opened directly onto the street, and each room had one barred window which was unglazed but in some cases covered with mosquito netting. The one door was both for security and nonsecretive access; there was no alley-entrance business and no slipping out the back way.

Thus, the girls sat in plain view at their open doors, or they stood about, alone or in small groups, chattering and laughing; if they had troubles, they kept them to themselves.

Many of the girls made a practice of sitting at their doors crocheting fine lace or embroidering dainty handkerchiefs. It was a maneuver that never failed. It reminded men who were perhaps having to spend long stretches of time in a foreign country or who had been at sea, in the jungle, the oil field, or the bush for weeks or months on end of the cozy domesticity of their homes.

A man couldn't pass a door without being greeted by a girl, who invited him with the sweetest of words and gestures to step in and have a good time. Often the invitation was accompanied by such daring promises that the most iron resistance and most holy vow might be overthrown on the spot. Once you had passed by her door, however, the girl would immediately desist, for you would be on her neighbor's territory where only she had a right to make inviting promises.

There was only one way to pass by these girls easily: "No money," and you were free to pass, assuming that the girl believed you. In most cases she didn't, but would playfully proceed to reach into your pockets, never actually lifting as much as a quinto.

The señoritas demonstrated their diplomacy in refraining from coaxing the local, respectable citizens who had to pass through the quarter on their way home. Most of them chose their clients according to their own tastes and by no means accosted every man who passed their door. A man might pause at a door, intent on getting on with a particular girl, but no amount of money or high bidding could win her over if for some reason the gentleman was not to her liking. Some señoritas refused to welcome a Chinese, others a Negro, and some wouldn't accept an Indian. Yet, as in all businesses, if trade was bad the girls might bring themselves to smile at someone whom three days previously they would have indignantly turned away.

The señoritas gave full value for the money. Yet these mistresses lacked what has been called the love of the adored woman. Time is money, and at the quarter you would search in vain for sweet trifling, for tender playfulness, for hours of desire and groping toward fulfillment. They had high art, yes; what you didn't get from them was the sweet longing for the lover.

Thus, the girls merely confirmed the priceless value of the loved and loving woman. They knew this, too, and made no attempt to deny it; they sold only and precisely what the gentlemen bargained for. They were artists and good business-women; they knew how to attract their clientele and how to keep the business going.

17

"Oh, now, there you are, Antonio," I greeted him. "I've been looking for you all around the quarter. I thought you must have gone home."

"No, I wasn't thinking of going home yet, Gales. Let's go to the Salón Pacífico and try our luck."

The Pacífico had a broad main room decorated in gold. Along one side were a number of recesses, each with a table surrounded on three sides by a comfortably padded bench; the back wall had a similar settee along its entire length. Opposite the recesses was a bar with high stools, and on a platform in the corner was the dance band. The walls were decorated with life-size paintings of nude women. These handsome women needed no fig leaves to remind you that they had something to hide. In this country it would be laughable to try to persuade men and women or even children that the human body sprouted fig leaves.

The girls were sitting on the long settee waiting for dancing partners, while the men sat at the bar or in the recesses. Two or three men had girls with them and were conversing with great decorum and with as much animation as if they were in a ballroom of New York's upper set. But they were enjoying themselves more because they could, if they so wished, say what was in their hearts, whereas in the upper set such talk might lead others to suspect that you didn't know the niceties of the language.

A one-step dance piece was blaring from the platform, but the men were slow to react; they seemed embarrassed and shy, and if the girls hadn't given them such friendly and encouraging smiles they never would have brought themselves to dance. They tried to conceal their shyness by sitting at the bar and drinking and drinking, drinking more than they really wanted. It was their way of showing their manliness, for they lacked the courage to show it in any other way. They went on drinking so as to be able to stay in the Pacífico near the girls whose smiles they loved and whose pretty faces they were delighted to see. But despite the smiles of the girls, the men held back and obliged the girls to dance with each other. Finally, a few men plucked up courage and asked a señorita for a dance. Then others began to unbend a little.

After a dance, the men as a rule escorted their partners back to their seats while they themselves went to the bar or to a seat in the recesses; but now and again a gentleman might invite one or two—if he didn't feel confident, three or four—girls to share his table and drink a bottle of beer or take a shot of something stronger.

"What will you have to drink, señorita?"

"A whiskey and soda for me."

"I'll have a cognac."

"For me, a bacardi."

"I'll have a bottle of beer."

"I'd like a pack of cigarettes."

They never ordered champagne or expensive wines on such easy invitation, but if a man happened to be there who felt like showing off or was bent on getting through four months' wages in one night, he would order champagne and goodness knows what else and issue the invitation, "It's on me, seño-ritas!" Twenty or more of them might then join in the spree, and things would warm up. On such occasions nothing was forbidden and there was no closing time.

The proprietor had his legal license, all stamped and hung up in plain sight, to manage his business so that it did not run at a loss. To avoid misunderstanding, he had signs hung up, such as "All Drinks One Peso." There was no need for police regula-tion, in price or anything else. The customers and proprietors regulated things between themselves by the free play of supply and demand, through free competition, and the absence of conditions imposed by overrestrictive licenses. If too many bars opened there was no need for the authorities to intervene; the ones that were superfluous went broke of their own accord. Only the ones that gave good value for their money survived.

Antonio and I had taken a table when we came in. We ordered beer. Then we danced with two girls and invited them to sit with us; they ordered whiskey. We didn't quite know what to say to them, and I felt sorry for them while they were making every effort to get a conversation going. I was glad when another dance started; we could make more progress with our feet than with our tongues.

For the sake of talking, we asked them all sorts of silly questions. Did they have to see their health doctors every week or every two weeks? Did those who didn't dance in the cafés have to pay more rent for their apartments than the dancers? What were their earnings?

They must have thought us very green to be asking such silly questions, when we might have been talking about more interesting things. But their amiable manner didn't desert them; it couldn't, for they couldn't allow themselves the luxury of moods and pouts, which would be bad for their business.

"Will you have another of the same to drink, señorita?" I asked the girl with whom I had danced.

"Thank you, señor, that will be fine."

"Then I'll order," I said.

There she sat, and after a few sips of the drink I had ordered, the girl started a conversation.

"I'm from Charlottenburg," began Jeannette.

"Oh, I thought you were a Parisienne," said I.

She was flattered. The genuine French girls, she said, called her "Boche" when they were having one of their frequent rows. Her real name was Olga, but she had her health certificate in the name of Jeannette, with a photo to authenticate it.

Jeannette had lived in Buenos Aires during the war of 1914–1918. She had been very active in her profession there and had made a small fortune.

"I suddenly got the urge to go back home and see what it looked like," she told me.

She found her father and mother living in the most pitiful circumstances. Before the war her father had been with a big Berlin firm as factory doorman, but had been dismissed after the war because a disabled veteran had been given preference.

Her father and mother had lived poorly all their lives, saving and saving for their old age, investing their money in government savings bonds; but when the government devalued the currency, and thus cheated orphans, widows, servant girls, and honest old folks out of their savings so unscrupulously that if any private individual had dared to do it he would have been publicly branded and perhaps imprisoned, the supposedly gilt-edged security of the Bartels family—Jeannette told me this was her German family name, though I didn't believe it—became scraps of paper so worthless that they couldn't even have been put to good use in an outhouse.

The Bartels decided to gas themselves, but just at that point they received a two-week supply of groats, rice, and dried vegetables along with a tin of corned beef from some charitable organization, and with this they kept body and soul together for another four weeks.

Then one fine afternoon Jeannette arrived without warning, having traveled from Buenos Aires to Hamburg. She brought with her so much money that she could have bought up a whole street in Charlottenburg, for she had dollars from the New World.

"My dear girl, how did you come by so much money?" her mother asked.

"I married a cattle rancher in the Argentine. He owned two million head of cattle, and when he died he left me a little fortune."

"Whoever would have thought that my girl would have such a stroke of luck?" said the mother. Thus, Jeannette was known in the neighborhood as the Argentine millionaire's widow.

With a handful of dollars, Jeannette bought her parents an apartment house that before the war had been worth maybe a half million marks. She had the title made out in her own name, so businesslike had she become in the New World, but her parents were assigned the income from the apartment house. Then she bought them a good number of sound shares that would move with the stock market prices; these she deposited with a dependable banking firm, with instructions that the dividends when due were to be paid to her parents.

This business over, Jeannette took a few weeks off to treat herself to a good time, which she well deserved after the strenuous years that lay behind her.

For the proper enjoyment of these weeks of pleasure the cooperation of the opposite sex was, of course, required. Pleasure is barely conceivable without it. But Jeannette didn't make it a matter of her professional business; being on vacation, she carefully chose a gentleman with whom she knew she could enjoy herself.

The Bartels had moved into the apartment house; with official permission from the housing authorities they were allowed to occupy the flat on the top floor, which Jeannette had had built at her own expense. One morning Father Bartel went to Jeannette's bedroom to speak to her and found her in bed with a gentleman. Jeannette and her friend had sat up late in a cabaret, drinking plenty of champagne, and for that reason he had not wakened in time to take his leave at a respectable early hour, in propriety and silence.

Father Bartel wanted to beat up the man, or shoot him, or deal with him in some other drastic manner. The gentleman, however, was tactful and well-bred; so with supreme dexterity he succeeded, despite Bartel's aggressions, in getting himself more or less dressed. Then, with Jeannette's help, he maneuvered himself to the door, onto the stairway, and away. He was safe.

Not so Jeannette. Her father, no longer obliged to deploy his forces on two fronts, gave her the full fury of his anger.

"Why did you come here, you whore, and shame us in front of everyone?" he roared at his daughter. "Better I'd have committed suicide as an honest doorman than to be so disgraced by my own daughter. You're nothing but a whore, damn you. I'm done with you! Leave my house at once!"

The mother tried to calm him, but only made matters worse. The old man was furious, for the honor of a factory doorman had been trampled into the dirt. He had, as he insisted a hundred times, grown old with honor, and now when he had one foot in the grave, he had to suffer humiliation at the hands of his own daughter whom he had always regarded as an angel from heaven.

Jeannette listened to all this in silence. It seemed to her so remote, so strange, and indescribably silly that she felt it was all taking place on a stage, and that she was in the audience watching an old-fashioned piece of melodrama.

When Father Bartel repeated for the third time, "Never darken my door again, you're my daughter no longer!" she suddenly realized that he was speaking to her.

Then she let him have it. She didn't get worked up, but told him in a lively, conversational tone: "Not your daughter? Maybe you were responsible for bringing me into the world, but I didn't ask you to, and I don't think I'd have chosen you if I'd been consulted. What right have you to turn me out of this house? A fine father! No one ever called me a whore before. If any man had, I'd have clawed his face into shreds. Only my own father takes it upon himself to call me a whore! Anyhow, there's no misunderstanding; you're right! I'm just what you say. And what you are living on now are whore's earnings!"

The father was silent. He just stared at her. The mother meanwhile sat down and cried quietly to herself. As a woman, with finer perceptions largely denied to men, she already had suspected the truth. But her homely common sense acquired over a lifetime of hard work had taught her not to probe needlessly into things which are best left alone. She thought it wiser not to know the precise truth; that way, life was easier to bear.

Jeannette was anxious to put her cards on the table and be done with it. Her role as a millionaire's widow hadn't been to her liking from the first, but the words had been put into her mouth by persistent questions on the origin of her riches. Now she was sick of the pose, even for the short time she meant to be in Charlottenburg.

"Yes, whore's earnings," she repeated with emphasis. "Every two, three, or four dollars means one man. Now you can figure out for yourself how many I've had and how many it took to save you from gassing yourselves. And as to your honorable watchman's life, it's no great honor to be buried a suicide! But of all the men who came to me not one ever called me a whore, not even the drunks, not even the sailors who come from long voyages and carry on like young bulls. All of them have said a friendly and courteous "Goodnight" when they left me, and most of them added a polite and genuine, "Thank you, señorita." And why? Because I never cheated anyone. What you call honor isn't my kind of honor; my honor and my pride are that everyone who comes to me gets an honest deal. I've always been worth the money, and today with all my experience I'm worth it more than ever. That is my pride and honor, never to cheat anyone.

"All right then, I'm a whore! But I've got money, while you with your watchman's honor have none. Nobody will give you anything for your honor. And if I don't give you spending money you hang around the place here all day and make Mother's life a hell with your moaning. If it'll give you any pleasure, you're welcome to run out in the street and tell everyone that the Argentine millionaire's widow is a whore! I don't care. I just don't give a damn. I've already got my visa, and I hadn't thought of going this month, but now I'll be off in an hour. I can still have a good time for a few weeks in Scheveningen and Ostende—I can afford it. Then I'll start work again. I need another fifteen thousand to reach my goal. And now, please leave me alone. I'm going to dress and pack my trunks."

Father Bartel left the room like a robot, and Jeannette said to her mother, "Look after Father. Don't leave him alone; he might do something silly." So the mother left. Jeannette packed quickly; within half an hour she stood in the hallway with her trunks packed and locked. She went down to the fourth floor to phone for a taxi.

Before the old couple had time to recover their senses, the taxi driver was tooting, and Jeannette called to him to come for her trunks. She took two hundred dollars from her handbag, put it on the table, and kissed her mother good-bye. Then calmly she took her father's head between her hands, kissed him and said, "Good-bye, Father dear. Don't think too badly of me, and don't make a tragedy of it. Understand, I might otherwise have died of typhoid. I needed money for typhoid shots and hospital treatment, and that was how it all started. When I recovered, I was too weak to work, and so the whole thing went on. It saved my life, and both of yours. So . . . Now you know everything and can figure out the details for yourself. Well, good-bye. Who knows whether I'll see you again in this life?"

The old father started to cry, took her in his arms, kissed her, and said, "Good-bye, child. I'm old, that's all. It's all right. You know best. Write us some time; Mother and I will be glad, always, to hear a word from you."

Then she was off. In time the old folks came to terms with the immoral earnings, and Jeannette sent money to them every quarter, which they never refused. Honor remains upright only if you don't have to starve; for a sense of honor depends on the number of meals you eat each day, how many you would like to eat, and how many you don't eat. That's why there are three categories and three different conceptions of honor.

"And then," Jeannette continued with her story, "I went to Santiago, Chile, then to Lima, Peru, and eventually came here. You have to know the ropes and understand men if you want to do business here. Competition is keen."

"But you can't go on doing this forever," I said.

"Of course not. The saddest thing in this world is an old

lady sitting in front of her door or walking the streets and lending herself to actions which we young ones would refuse with a wave of the hand. I'll stay in this business until I'm thirty-six, and then I'll quit. I've saved my money, never gone in for the high life and big spending. Would you like to know how my account stands with the American bank here? You'd never believe it!—besides, it doesn't matter. Later on I'll buy myself a small estate in Germany or a farm in Canada, and then I'll get married."

"Married?"

"Why not? Of course I'll marry, at thirty-six, for that's when a woman really begins to enjoy life; and I mean to make something of my life and my marriage. After all, I have experience and I understand men, and I'll give my husband such a life and such a bed that he'll appreciate what a treasure he has in me."

"But you're taking a big risk, Jeannette. The world is small, very small, and a chance meeting with a—let's be frank!— three-dollar or five-dollar acquaintance might wreck your marriage!"

Jeannette laughed. "Not in my case. You don't know me, yet! As I said to my father: My honor is that I never cheat anyone, least of all my husband when I have one. Before we ever come to a mutual agreement, I'll tell him frankly how I got my money. If he rises above it, I'll say, 'All right, then, we'll get married under these conditions: that you'll never reproach me as to how I got my fortune, and that I'll never reproach you for taking it easy on my money!'

"I'll keep the money, but he'll get enough so as not to have to ask me for every penny. And I'll give him a trial run beforehand, just to make sure that I'm not betting on the wrong horse!"

So ended her story.

And the man who gets Jeannette will have cause to be thankful. If he isn't a moral prig, he'll discover in a week, yes, or in a night, that Jeannette is worth five times her fortune, for she'll never let a marriage get dull. As I personally learned, Jeannette leaves no desires unfulfilled!

18

 We arrived at the bakehouse about half past eleven. In order to reach the dormitory, and change into our work clothes, we had to pass through the bakehouse, where the men were hard at work.

The master saw us, and pulled out his watch. "It's nearly twelve," he said.

"I know," I replied, "we've just seen the cathedral clock. And while we're at it, I might as well tell you that I'm through."

"Since when?"

"Since now."

"Then you'd better tell the old man. He's out front in the café."

"I know. You needn't tell me. I came in through the café."

"And I'm turning in my time, too," Antonio joined me.

"Why do you both have to leave?" asked the master.

"We're not a pair of suckers, to stay here and work eighteen hours a day," said Antonio.

"You've been drinking," said the master.

Antonio got belligerent: "What did you say?"

"Well, I ought to be allowed to say that it's nearly twelve,"

151

the master retorted. "We've been here working since ten, there's so much to do."

"You may say what you please, but not to us," I put in. "You're not our boss now."

"All right," said the master. "If that's how it is, clear out at once. You needn't sleep here, and there won't be any breakfast for you in the morning, either."

"We didn't ask you for any," Antonio replied, "and if we did want breakfast we wouldn't come to you for the favor."

With that, we went to the dormitory, stuffed our working rags into an empty sugar sack, and were about to leave when Antonio suddenly remembered something.

"Wait. We've left our two pesos in the old shoe, and we'd better get them. We're not leaving our pesos for them to buy new pictures!"

We got our pesos and passed through the bakehouse once more.

"Who tore down the pictures?" asked the Czech.

"We did. Any objections?" Antonio snapped. "Speak up. We're just in the mood. We sure ought to be able to do as we please with our own pictures."

"I didn't know that they belonged to you. Anyhow, you needn't have torn them up," said another worker.

"I don't like indecent pictures," Antonio replied. "If you must have stuff like that staring you in the face, you can buy it for yourselves. We don't need such pictures, do we, Gales?"

"Not us! I'm glad to say that we don't." I spoke with great conviction.

Then we went to Doux and asked for the money that was due us. "Come back tomorrow," he told us.

"We know all about your tomorrows," we said.

Antonio put his sack on the floor, leaned over the counter toward Doux, and raised his voice: "Will you give us our money now, or won't you? Or must we call the police to make you pay us the wages we've earned?"

"Don't shout like that, or the customers will hear you," said Doux quietly, putting his hand in his pocket. "I'll pay you. I've never owed one centavo for wages. Would you like a bottle of beer?"

"I don't mind if I do," replied Antonio. "We're not too proud to accept it."

We sat at a table and a waiter served us the beer.

"We don't want to make Doux a present of the beer, the old skinflint," I said. "He seemed to think we'd say no, or he'd never have offered it to us."

"Sure," said Antonio. "That's why I said yes, though I didn't really want it!"

Doux didn't ask us why we were leaving. These sudden departures were the norm here; he took no notice of them, and didn't try to persuade us to stay, for he knew from experience that it would have been useless.

He went to the cash box and then brought over our money, put it down on the table, and disappeared behind the counter without another word or another look in our direction.

Antonio and I went to a coffee stall where we drank a glass of coffee and where the woman in charge allowed us to leave our sacks until the next morning, when we would return for breakfast. Then we went back to the girls, where life was more pleasant than in the bakehouse.

The next day, after a morning of loafing on benches in the plaza, we went to a boardinghouse, where we each reserved a bed for fifty centavos and deposited our bags in the baggage room.

Our names were duly registered and we were given room and bed numbers. Each room had six to eight beds, which were placed at random where there happened to be space for them.

Baths were available at any hour, day or night—shower baths at twenty-five centavos each. For this you got soap, towel, and a piece of rafia—a sort of straw washcloth. There was no faucet to regulate the flow of water, but a chain pull, forcing you to bathe with one hand while the other hand kept pulling the chain so the water would run. If you soaped yourself with both hands, the water would stop; this saved water, of course. After taking a shower we lay down for a long siesta.

About eight in the evening we got up and went into town again, planning to return later. We stopped at a bar. A tall man was standing around drinking tequila; he wore riding boots and spurs, his face was rough, and he sported a mighty mustache.

"Hi, there!" he called as we were going out. "Are you looking for work?"

"Maybe. What sort? Where?"

"Cotton-picking. In Concordia, for Mr. G. Mason. Usual pickers' pay, and it's near the railroad. The fare's only three pesos sixty."

"Are you authorized to hire?"

"Of course. Otherwise I wouldn't be telling you."

"All right. Let me have it on a slip of paper."

He got himself a slip of paper from the bartender, then took a stump of a pencil from his shirt pocket and scribbled something on the paper.

I read the note: "Mr. G. Mason, Concordia. This man has come for the picking. L. Wood."

I talked the matter of the job over with Antonio, but he decided against it. So the next morning I left Antonio at the boardinghouse and took the train to Concordia.

When I arrived I found Mr. Mason right away; he was in the field where many pickers were already busy and the work was well underway. But when Mr. Mason saw my note, he said: "L. Wood? Don't know him. Never told him to send pickers to me. Don't need any. I've got enough."

"But you are Mr. G. Mason?"

"No, I am W. Mason."

"Does a G. Mason live around here?" I asked.

"No."

"Then it must mean you. The G must be a mistake, since you are picking here. How can that Mr. Wood, if that's his real name, know that a Mr. Mason lives here and is just starting to pick cotton?"

The farmer looked doubtful. "I've no idea, no more than you. Anyhow, I don't know anyone named Wood, and my first name begins with W not G."

"This is a fine business," I said, "making a fellow spend railway fare when he's practically broke to start with. I'll tell you something, Mr. Mason, there's something wrong here. Someone has done me out of my time and money."

"Well, you can start picking here if you like," Mr. Mason relented now, "but it won't be worth your effort. I've got only natives picking, and they do it cheap, very, very cheap. And there's no place for you to live around here."

"I don't need a blueprint to see how things are," I said.

"Have you ever worked as a carpenter?"

"I'm an experienced joiner."

If you don't want to starve in that part of the world you have to be able to do anything. I hadn't the faintest idea of carpentry, but I thought that once I was confronted with the job and had a tool in my hand, the rest would follow automatically.

"If you're a carpenter, I can get work for you," said Mr. Mason. "There's a farmer who's building himself a new house, and he can't get on with it because he doesn't know anything about joinery. I'll give you a note to him. He's only an hour's hike from the station."

I wasn't born yesterday. I knew perfectly well that no farmer wanted a carpenter and that Mr. Mason was only planning to get rid of me before I insisted that he pay my fare. No doubt he'd instructed Mr. Wood to send pickers to him, and meanwhile he'd hired Indian pickers for less money. That's the kind of tricks they pull on the unemployed; they recruited men all over the area, not being sure how many would turn up. Wherever the farmers had friends or acquaintances they'd send word for pickers, and there were always those dupes and down-and-outers who'd risk their last peso on the train fare. Then the farmer would choose the cheapest workers and, what's more, he'd beat down the pickers' wages; for the migrant worker wouldn't have the money to get away again and would be forced to pick for as little as three centavos the kilo.

There was no point in my arguing with Mason, for the only way to settle accounts with him would have been to push his face in; but he had a gun in his back pocket, and no matter how well I aimed my fists they were no match for nickel-plated bullets.

So I had to go back to the station, and while there I thought I might as well call on the farmer. It was just as I'd thought; he didn't want a carpenter, for he was carpenter enough himself to have built a good solid house with the help of three natives. However, my asking for a job got me a good meal. And the farmer confirmed that Mason was the meanest kind of welcher and pulled the same dirty trick every year, so that an influx of whites looking for work enabled him to cut the natives' wages to rock bottom. For these poor fellows, who had hardly any other income during the whole year, resigned themselves to the constant lowering of their wages when they saw that even white men were begging for the job of picking cotton.

19

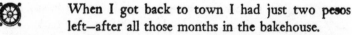

When I got back to town I had just two pesos
left—after all those months in the bakehouse.

I went to the boardinghouse, where I hoped to find Antonio,
but he wasn't there. He never went to bed before twelve, for
life was at its best in the cool evening when pretty girls
promenaded in the plaza while the band played. So I went in
search of him.

Unable to find him in any of the plazas, I thought that he
might be at the gambling joint. It was on the upper floor of a
certain large house which had a bar on the ground floor. No
drinks were sold in the gambling salons, but ice water could be
had, gratis. I went in just as I was, without vest or jacket, for
the owners and managers weren't concerned with what customers had on their backs, but with what they had in their
pockets. A man in a work shirt might have two or three
months' oil driller's wages in his work pants. The more grease-
stained and muddied his trousers, his shirt and hat and boots,
the more likely it was that he had two or three thousand pesos
on him and had come to the joint to try to double the amount.

On the landing two men sat at a small table and watched
everyone who went upstairs. They knew every customer who

157

had been there before and had a good memory for the faces of those who weren't allowed to enter because of past misbehavior. If a customer claimed that a croupier had defrauded him, the croupier would pay out the ten or twenty pesos in question without a word of argument, despite the fact that the bank was in the right; but the gambler would never be allowed in the place again.

Cards and dice were promptly changed if a player showed the slightest suspicion that he was losing by some sort of manipulation; but, in fact, the bank never cheated. If anyone cheated, it was the guests. The bank knew that it was good business to play absolutely straight.

The gambling hall was jammed, and if it hadn't been for the many fans and ventilators, the heat would have made any long stay impossible. There were roulette tables, poker tables, baccarat, and even "seventeen and four" games. One bank was kept by a Chinese who was a member of the board. This place was called the Jockey Club, and it was open to members only; handily enough, you became a member when you entered. Though the law required that every player hold a membership card, no one was ever asked to show his card, certainly never a white man.

I had guessed right. Antonio was there. He was standing at a dice table, where a "steerer," paid to stimulate interest at empty tables, was playing. The steerer was raising his stake at every throw, until at last he was staking twenty-five pesos at a time, and this attracted the attention of the guests who were at other tables. People were intrigued by the high stake; they pressed nearer; they crowded around to watch the reckless player. Naturally the steerer had ordinary gambler's luck, but it wasn't his own money at stake; it was the bank's. The less-experienced guests, of course, didn't know that the fellow was a steerer. So, within a few minutes, the table was besieged by a dozen excited men watching the fall of the dice and mentally calculating combinations and intervals at which the numbers were recurring. As soon as they felt that they had figured out the combinations they started playing; so the dice table, which had been empty ten minutes earlier, with only the croupier standing by it, was now the center of attention. Every square was taken, three or four times over.

This drained the baccarat table of players and gave its croupier a chance to make up his accounts, exchange chips, and stack up a new pack of cards. When he was all set again, and the croupier at the dice table was beginning to sweat, two steerers came and started to play at the baccarat table. Gradually the dice game slowed down, while the crowd at the baccarat table increased.

In one corner a bank was being auctioned; the bidding started at five pesos, the next bid was ten, and it finally went for sixty pesos. I looked over at the man who had bought it.

"Damn it all, Leary, old boy, what are you doing here?" I called, for I'd worked with Leary at the oil camp. "I'll cross my fingers for you, Leary, up to three hundred. Agreed?" I shouted.

"Agreed, Gales," he called back.

The people who had heard us laughed and came over to the table where Leary sat down to take over his bank. The play started. Leary had to bleed—a hundred, two hundred, three hundred. He shelled out the money in stacks and pushed it to the winners. He had run out of chips.

"Damn it, Gales, what's up?"

"Don't worry, Leary, throw in all you've got!"

"All right, I'll do it," Leary called over, "but I'll be after your blood if I'm left in the lurch."

"Keep it up. I'm good for three hundred by gentlemen's agreement." I had two pesos in my pocket.

Leary went ahead with the bets—four hundred, five hundred, six hundred, seven hundred. His face was as red as a tomato, and he looked as if he were about to burst; he pulled out a handkerchief and wiped streaming sweat from his face.

The cards fell once again. His bank won. I squeezed my fingers hard. The bank won again. Leary got up. "I'm auctioning off this bank," he announced.

"How much have you made, Leary?" I asked him when we met and shook hands in the crowd.

"Made? How much? I don't know exactly. But here, take this, it's yours," and he gave me two hundred pesos.

I'd certainly earned it. But he didn't tell me how much he'd made; he must have tucked away a tidy roll.

Easy come, easy go. But these two hundred pesos hadn't been so easy, and I took good care of them. I lent Antonio fifteen pesos so he could rent a cigarette stall and stock it; the rent for the tiny booth with a striped awning to keep off the hot sun was nine pesos a month.

The daily tax on Antonio's stall was fifteen centavos. The municipal collector came along every morning to collect it, giving Antonio a stamped receipt which had to be shown when another official appeared in the afternoon to collect from those who hadn't paid in the morning. This small daily tax was all you had to pay the authorities to set up shop in the street.

If business was going badly, Antonio would say to the collector: "I've hardly earned my lunch today," and the collector would waive the tax for that day. He believed the street trader's claim of poor business, just as the trader believed him if on some other occasion he had something out of the ordinary to say. Trust for trust.

Actually, Antonio didn't make much. One day one peso; another, two pesos—seldom more than two. But it was easier than the bakehouse, although the working hours were as long. Sometimes Antonio stayed at his stall from five in the morning until midnight.

I got one or two packs of cigarettes from him every day and

so reduced his debt to me. It took a long time, for each pack cost only ten centavos. Some packets contained premiums for ten, twenty, or fifty centavos, which Antonio had to pay out of his own pocket. Eventually the manufacturers refunded these amounts, but the outlay was hard on Antonio.

One afternoon when I was reminiscing with him, sitting on a packing box by his stall, I asked him: "Why didn't you come cotton-picking with me that time? You had the fare, the same as I did."

"That's it, I had the fare. That's why I didn't come! I warned you, but you didn't believe me. You'll not be taken in so easily again."

"You never can tell in advance whether or not it's the real thing. Last year it was," I reminded him.

"Yes, of course, it may be the real thing, fair work and proper picker's pay, but I've had enough of that. Three years ago I went picking, and do you know what happened?"

"What?"

"When the first week was over, we asked for our wages, but the farmer said that he could advance us only one peso each, which of course wasn't enough to buy the food we needed for the coming week. He could not advance us one centavo more, he said, because he had no money; but if we needed any supplies we could get them from his store. So we got food from him because we had to eat. From that day on, he gave us no cash, but only I.O.U.'s on his store, charging us about twice as much for the stuff we bought as we'd have had to pay in town. Eighty-centavo tobacco went for one peso forty in his store. A three-peso shirt was six pesos. And it was the same with coffee, flour, beans—everything. When all the cotton was in and we wanted to settle our account and get our wages, he told us quite brazenly that he had no money himself and that we could have goods and supplies for the money owing us. But what could we have done with the goods? We needed money to get back to town."

"Did you ever get the money, Antonio?"

"No. When we left, we had to walk. He said we should write and give our addresses so he could send the money in October. He never sent a single centavo, and still owes us the wages to this day. So we picked for those eight weeks for nothing."

"Well, there's nothing you can do about it now," I said. "They still use the same tactics as during the dictatorship of Diaz. But don't worry, Antonio, there'll be an end to this some day before the Revolution is completely over!"

"I don't know. They can always get more men; but different ones, for there's always a new crop of suckers every season, men who know they'll starve if they stay in town, men who want to work at an honest job. Things may improve, though. We've got good governors in a few of the states now, elected by the workers, in San Luis Potosí and here in Tamaulipas, for example. The governors spoke at a workers' meeting not long ago and promised action. The governor of this state is preparing a regulation whereby every cotton farmer will have to deposit twenty-five pesos for every picker, and pay his return fare. So that's a start.

"So far, Gales, the farmers have been able to do what they pleased with us poor devils. And when they can't get any pickers they'll go around moaning about the harvest rotting on their hands, and they'll say that the Agricultural Workers' Union is to blame and ought to be disbanded. Then they talk about the good-for-nothing Indians and the peons who'd rather live as bandits than do an honest day's work. No one can take me in with that bunk. Cotton-picking? Me? What sort of fool do you take me for? I'd as soon be pushing up daisies. Or rob. Have you ever seen a poor farmer here? I haven't. He might have some hard going for the first three years, but once he's worked up his land it's safer than a gold mine. And they're not satisfied with that; they want to turn it into a diamond mine by cheating the workers out of their wages. Cabrones!"

Antonio was right. I made up my mind to bring my career as a cotton-picker to an end, once and for all. There was nothing to be got out of it, so it was pointless. What was Europe's cotton consumption to me? If they wanted cotton over there, let them come over and pick it themselves; then they'd know what it meant to pick cotton. Heavy with this newly gained worldly wisdom I left Antonio's stall and went over to the snack bar for some coffee and French rolls.

20

   Next to me in the snack bar was an American, an
elderly man, and obviously a rancher.

"Are you looking for something?" he asked.

"Yes, the sugar!"

He passed me the enameled bowl.

"I didn't mean that," he said, smiling. "What I meant was,
would you like to earn some money?"

"I always like earning money," I replied.

"Have you ever cut out cattle?"

"I grew up on a cattle farm."

"Then I've got a job for you!"

"Really?"

"A thousand head of cattle, sixty heavy bulls among them,
to be driven three hundred and fifty miles overland from my
ranch to the port. We leave for the ranch tomorrow morning."

"Agreed!" I shook his hand. "Where can we make the
contract?"

"Hotel Palacio. At five. In the lobby."

These cattle couldn't be transported by rail; there were no
facilities for that, neither cattle cars nor loading points. As to
overland drive there existed only few roads, many mountain

ranges had to be crossed, swamps bypassed, rivers forded. Grazing pasture and water had to be found every day.

"Three hundred and fifty miles?" I asked the rancher when we met to talk it over. "As the crow flies?"

"Yes, as the crow flies," said the rancher. Mr. Pratt was his name.

"Dammit, that might turn out to be six hundred."

"Not so unlikely. Still, as far as I've figured, it might be possible to keep a fairly direct route."

"What about pay?"

"Six pesos a day. I provide horse, saddle, and equipment. You cook your own food on the way. I'll send along six of my men whom the animals are well used to—Indians. The foreman, a Mestizo, will also go with you. He's quite a good man, reliable. I might perhaps trust him with the herd—but no. If he'd sell the herd on the way, and bolt, I could do nothing about it. His wife and children live on my ranch, but that's no security! You could search for the likes of him forevermore in this country. Besides, I wouldn't like to give him so much money to carry about; on the other hand, I couldn't send him off without money. There are so many expenses on the drive and it's not fair to tempt any man that way. As for me, I can't stay away from the rancho that long. The bandits'd be around the place before you could say *knife*. That's why I'd like to get hold of a gringo like you to take over the drive."

"Well, I don't know if I'm as honest as you think. Not yet, anyhow," I said with a laugh. "I, too, know how to bolt with a herd. After all, you've just picked me up in the street."

"I judge a man by his face," Mr. Pratt went on; then, after a pause, "to be perfectly honest, I'm not trusting entirely to luck. I know you."

"You know me? I can't imagine how."

"Didn't you work for a farmer Shine?"

"Yes."

"I saw you there. And I have Mr. Shine's word that I can rely on you. So you'll have the contract, you'll drive the herd, and I'll advance you money to pay your daily expenses."

"Very well! But what about the contract bonus?"

Mr. Pratt was silent for a while, then took out his notebook, made a few calculations, and said: "I've leased pastureland near the port, two miles from the main terminal market. It's well fenced. There I can wait for cattle buyers to come to me, and I'll probably get orders for several shiploads. If not, I'll sell the herd in small lots. I've got a good and very reliable agent there who's been working with me for years, and has always got good prices——"

"That's all very well," I interjected, "but what about my contract and bonus?"

"All right. For each head that you drive through, sound from horn to hoof, I'll pay you sixty centavos extra. If your losses are less than two percent, I'll give you a hundred-peso bonus on top of that, plus your pay."

"What about the losses?"

"I'll deduct twenty-five pesos for every head lost above two percent," said Mr. Pratt.

"Just a moment," I broke in. I made a few quick calculations myself on the margin of a newspaper. "Sold," I agreed. "Let me have a note of the contract."

He tore a leaf out of his little notebook, wrote the conditions of our contract in pencil, signed it and handed it to me. "Your address?" he asked.

"My address? That's an awkward point!" (I really didn't have an address.) "Let's say right here, Hotel Palacio."

"Okay. All right."

"How do matters stand at present? Has the herd been cut out?"

"No, not a single head has been cut out yet. There'll be a few yearlings, but most of the herd'll be two- and three-year-olds. Yes, a few four-year-olds, too. I'll help you cut them out."

"All branded?"

"All of them. No trouble there."

"What about the leader bulls?"

"That's your problem. You'll have to see about them."

"All right by me. I can manage to pick them."

Mr. Pratt got up. "Now let's have a drink, and then you're going to have dinner with me. Afterward, I've got some private business to attend to."

What his private business was, that was no concern of mine. I'm not curious when it comes to private business. One of the many reasons why I am still alive.

When we parted after dinner, Mr. Pratt asked how much advance I wanted. "Nothing," I said.

"What? You don't need an advance?" He acted astonished. "That sounds funny. Where did you come by your cash on hand?"

"In the gambling casino."

"Huh! I'll have a go at it myself, Gales, later tonight. Maybe I can win your wages and bonus."

"You won't win them from me, Mr. Pratt. You won't even see me there, for I mean to keep what I've got."

"I wouldn't want to win money off you, Gales. I'll win it off the others. There're always a few crazy ones in from the oil camps who can't get rid of their cash quick enough. I'll make a solo table with two or three of them. If you want to learn how it's done, come along and watch me."

"No, thanks, not interested!" I said, and went on my way.

21

 The next morning at five we boarded the train, a sixteen-hour express ride to the Pratt ranch ahead of us. I knew I'd be doing well if I drove the cattle back to the terminal in twice sixteen days.

The express train was a good one, made in Europe. There were only two classes in the coaches, first and second, Mexico having less class distinction than some four-class countries of Europe. Here, a first-class ticket cost a little more than twice that of second class; but you traveled just as rapidly in second as in first, and second wasn't at all uncomfortable.

First-class seats were arranged in two rows with an aisle between, the passengers facing forward. In second class, where mostly the poorer natives traveled, benches ran along the sides of the coach and at right angles to the benches were more seats. All seats were innocent of upholstery; but most of the second-class passengers carried enough blankets and bundles to upholster theirs.

The huge locomotives were fired by oil, and they had to produce great power to cross some of the highest railroad grades in the world. Behind the oil-tank tender were the express and luggage coaches and the mail car. Then came two long second-class coaches, a great first-class coach, and at the end ran the Pullman sleeper.

At the head of the second-class coaches there was always a detachment of soldiers, twelve to eighteen men, rifles loaded, an officer in charge. This detachment was a necessay precaution against attacks from bandits; but in spite of the presence of soldiers, such attacks still occurred. The ensuing battles between soldiers and bandits often lasted several hours and involved a number of dead.

There were no such things as grade crossings with automatic signals, nor even signalmen. The train rushed at a mad speed through jungle, bush, and tilled valley, across upland prairies, and over the Sierra Madre Oriente, whose highest peaks are covered with perpetual snow. Bridges spanned wide gorges, forty, fifty, and two hundred yards deep and several miles long; the bridges were of wood trestle, and the train tore across them at terrific speed.

Nowhere was the railroad track fenced off, and cattle, horses, burros, mules, sheep, pigs, goats, and wild animals of all kinds roamed along it and sometimes grazed or dozed between the rails. The locomotive gave off a blood-curdling hoot to clear the track, and sometimes the animals would clear off, and of course at other times wouldn't budge until the train stopped and one of the soldiers got out and threw stones at them. Sometimes the beasts ran head-on into the locomotive, or were caught without warning around a curve; so that the railroad embankment all along the way was marked with animal skeletons on either side.

Now and then we came upon wounded beasts, their legs crushed or bodies torn open, lying waiting for death, thirsting, crazed, under the tropical sun. No passer-by would kill them and put them out of their misery, because their owner might be lurking within sight and be capable of dragging the do-gooder into court and getting him fined for unauthorized slaughter of his beasts to the tune of fifty or a hundred pesos, or more. If you were pretty sure that you were unobserved you might put your pistol in the animal's ear and put him out of his suffering; then you'd better take to your heels, pronto. It's costly, taking pity on animals.

All along the railroad the zopilotes, the vultures, squatted and waited for victims—dead burros, dogs, cats, pigs. On upland plains or coastal flats long stretches of the railroad served also for caravans of burros and mules, for the adjacent road was often swallowed by bush or rainy-season floods.

The railroad was mainly of one track. Large water towers, wooden tanks on trestles, had been erected about every twenty miles so that the engines could refill. At many small stations the train seldom came to a full stop. A mail bag would be slung out and another one shot in. Some ice blocks, which were packed around with wood shavings to retard melting and then sewn into burlap, were simply tossed out for the consignee to pick up.

Tickets could be bought at the various stations or on the train, costing 25 percent more on the train; an extra charge which didn't apply, however, if a station had no ticket office. Many stations weren't expected to sell tickets after five in the evening, in order that the ticket clerk be spared having money in his isolated office after dark, a thing which could cost him his life. After dark the tickets cost the normal price aboard the train. Enroute, the tickets were collected by a conductor who then tucked a small tab inscribed with the code of destination into the passenger's hat band, thus keeping account of his many passengers.

The soldiers usually sat about with their first-grade primers, trying to learn to read. They were all Indians and very few of them could read or write, but they were consumed with an ambition to learn. One would help the other, and when one had learned to write *eso* he would be full of eagerness to pass his accomplishment on to his fellows.

About eight o'clock our train stopped for breakfast at a station which looked almost like a lively township. Mr. Pratt and I got off the train and entered a typical station buffet— Chinese café, of course. In fact, it was hard to find an eating place anywhere that wasn't Chinese.

After breakfast we walked up and down the platform where dozens of hawkers swarmed, offering things you'd never have expected to find for sale on a railroad platform: parrots, tiger cubs, skins of grown tigers, live iguanas, flowers, song birds in handmade wicker cages, oranges, tomatoes, bananas, mangos, pineapples, sticks of sugar cane fresh from the field, candied fruits, tortillas, roast chicken, smoked fish, boiled giant crabs; bottles of coffee, lemonade, beer, wine, pulque. Ragged, barefoot Indian girls ran along the train to offer themselves as servant girls or cooks in households.

For the twenty-odd minutes of the train's stop, the station was like a fairground. Except for our train and the evening train, it dozed in a dead calm, but now it was enough to make your head spin. A freight train might come through and cause a slight stir among the railroad employees; but, without passengers getting on and off, the station was torpid and sleepy. Most of its daily life was centered on those lively twenty minutes or so when the morning train stood there; and any vendor who failed to do business during that time had failed for the whole day.

At noon we arrived at a bigger station where we stopped for about forty minutes for the midday meal. In the station buffet thirty places were already laid on several big tables and half the plates were already filled with soup, for a quick glance was enough to tell the proprietor how many diners to prepare for.

Then came the long, long exhausting afternoon through jungle, prairielike grassland, and bush. The train from the opposite direction that crossed with us at noon had brought the morning papers from the nearest city and these were sold on the train.

At nine in the evening we got out at Mr. Pratt's little home station. We stopped at the cantina, which was also the local post office. Mr. Pratt greeted the cantina owner, a Señor Gomez, and introduced me.

Regular cooked meals weren't to be had in a place like this, but you didn't have to go hungry; you could in fact get a wonderful meal together. We bought a can of Vancouver salmon, a few cans of Spanish sardines in fine olive oil, a few cans of Vienna sausages (made in Chicago), a package of Kraft cheese, and some crackers. There were no bread or rolls. Bread doesn't keep well in that climate; it turns hard, gets moldy, or is attacked by small red ants.

With our canned snack we had bottles of Señor Gomez's beer, and then went to work on his stock of tequila. After a while we were dead to the world, if not ripe for burial; so we went into the cantina's poolroom, ourselves in our blankets, and lay down on the floor to sleep. Señor Gomez had a softer bed. He went to his wife.

Thinking of a woman or of women in general—I can't remember which—I fell asleep; and by one woman in particular, I was awakened the next morning. The woman in question was Mrs. Pratt. She had driven the Ford in from the ranch to do some shopping at the cantina and there she found her husband, though she hadn't expected him, least of all on the floor of the poolroom, and in a well-soaked condition.

Since the beginning of time, the innocent have had to suffer. I was innocent, so I had to suffer. Mr. Pratt was the model husband, but I—whom he'd picked up in the gutter—was the bum who had tempted and beguiled him and led him astray.

For he, the good Mr. Pratt, would never have done such a thing on his own. Oh, no!

As we were leaving, Mr. Pratt gave Señor Gomez a wink. Men always understand a wink, particularly if the two men who share the wink are married men trying to live in peace with their wives.

"Well," declared Gomez, "you had so-and-so many cans of sardines, and the sausages, and cheese,"—again the wink—"and you had two small bottles of beer, and Mr. Gales had four and three tequilas. That does it. I've chalked up the drinks on your bill."

Mrs. Pratt was well satisfied with her husband. (He could settle with Gomez later for the twenty or thirty bottles we'd tossed into the corner of the room. His credit with Gomez was very good.) But I got such a dirty look from Mrs. Pratt that I seriously considered canceling the contract then and there. For I had to spend at least two weeks in Mrs. Pratt's house, while we were cutting out the herd for the drive, and what couldn't this lady do to me in that time?

Just think of it. I'd got her good, sober husband into such a condition that even now after several hours' sleep he was bleary-eyed and could hardly stand up straight. It's unwise to go drinking with married men. It never does any good. They're a race apart.

So I was quite relieved when Mrs. Pratt shoved her customarily sober husband into the Ford, seated herself behind the steering wheel, started up, and clanked off. That I was hired to go along with them didn't seem to worry her—let the bum walk. But the thought of the fourteen miles from the station to the ranch gave me such impetus that, as Mrs. Pratt was turning onto the main road, I sprinted after the Ford and dove head first into the open trunk. My dive, however, hadn't been deep enough to get all of me into the trunk, so that a good part of my length, legs and all, dangled outside. I suspect that the Indian workers along the way must have thought that I was a tailor's dummy which Mrs. Pratt had picked up at the station; or they may have thought that Mrs. Pratt had run over me and was transporting me out of sight to the ranch to be buried there.

When we arrived at the ranch no one took any notice of me. Mrs. Pratt drove the Ford into a thatched barn and went into the house with her husband, leaving me still sticking part way out of the trunk. After a while I dragged myself out of my uncomfortable position and moved into the upholstered front seat.

When I awoke the sun was low. Whether it was rising or setting I didn't know; I was a stranger here, trying to get my bearings, where the landscape seemed a bit unsteady.

"Hello, you down there, have you slept off your booze yet?" Mrs. Pratt called from the porch of the ranch house. "My old fool of a husband sure picked a fine type of man, I must say. I can just see you driving the cattle into the Panama Canal, you drunk! It's good that there is a canal there, or we'd be chasing after you to Brazil, or wherever you wind up with them. Come in here now and have something to eat."

I ate a little of everything so as not to upset the good woman still further. Mr. Pratt sat over his food and picked about in his plate, not looking up, acting as if he didn't know me, grunting when I spoke to him. I knew the dodge, that he'd told his wife that I'd led him on, and that he was through with me, but that as he'd already incurred expenses on my behalf he'd send me off with the herd and have nothing more to do with me.

When Mrs. Pratt went out into the kitchen for a moment, he said: "Listen, my boy, be a good sport and play the game. It'll all blow over by tomorrow. She's not a bad sort; really, she's a grand soul. Only she can't stand drinking." Suddenly his tone changed: "You shouldn't have kept on asking me to drink to the President, to the national flag, and then to the cattle! I told you beforehand that I didn't drink. But what could I do when you started drinking toasts? It wasn't fair!"

Well, well, well. What? What was this—oh, Mrs. Pratt had come back into the room, so he was putting on his act. And he sure knew how to do it. He'd thundered out these last few words to such effect that Mrs. Pratt settled herself stiffly onto her chair, as if to say, "There you are, see what a decent guy my husband is. He drinks only out of patriotism, while with you—it's pure depravity!"

After the meal we were graciously excused; I was shown to my bed and I lay down to sleep.

22

   The following morning, immediately after breakfast, we saddled up and rode out to the prairie to see if I could pick out a horse for myself. These horses were born, bred, and raised out in the wide open; there was no horse stable on Mr. Pratt's ranch. They were shaggy, long-maned and long-tailed, though rather small; and they galloped off at the mere scent of man.

Two or three times a year these horses were rounded up and driven into a corral close to the ranch. Here they were fed and watered, so as to get used to man; they were tied up, bridled, saddled, and eventually mounted before being turned loose again on the range. And thus, with patience and care, the horses were kept this side of remaining wild. The trainers were careful never to break the horse's spirit, or hurt his pride, or curb his natural mettle.

I picked out a horse, neither the wildest nor the tamest, but one which looked as if it would stand the strenuous trek. We closed in on him, lassoed him, and took him back to the ranch, where I left him to his peace, tied to a tree. Later, I threw him some grain, which he ignored; then some fresh grass, which he likewise declined. So I let him go hungry and thirsty overnight. In the morning, I brought him more grass; but he shied off, to the end of his rope. Then I put some water in front of him, which he immediately tipped over as he wasn't used to drinking from a bucket, for he'd drunk only from streamlets and rain pools.

In time I made him, or rather his hunger made him, feed and drink; and so he came to associate food with my presence. Within two days I could come up to him and pat him gently on the back. He trembled, but after a while the trembling ceased. I could not, of course not, spend all my time with the horse, only moments when we came to the rancho for meals; meanwhile we were very busy cutting out the herd.

When the horse had become used to me, I put a bitless bridle on him, with a bridle strap fastened outside around his mouth. If a horse hasn't been ruined by rough handling, you can ride him without any iron in the mouth; in fact, he responds wonderfully. The assumption that you can master a horse only if you tear its mouth open, or dig its sides raw with spurs, is utterly false.

At last I saddled him; and every time I came to the ranch to eat, I tightened the straps. At the same time I pressed the saddle and put weight on it as if I were going to mount. Then I let down the stirrups, so that they dangled freely and knocked against his flanks. Now I moved about as if to mount, by putting a boot in the stirrup. At the first attempt, he kicked and danced away; but in a few days he was well accustomed to the knocking and dangling of the stirrups. Then I jumped on, got one leg over the saddle, and jumped off again.

All this time the horse had been tied, sometimes on a long rope, sometimes on a short one. At last I ventured to mount. I blindfolded him and got into the saddle. He stood still and his whole body trembled. Quickly I jumped off, patted his neck and back, and kept up a flow of smooth talk. I mounted again. He turned, quivered, but danced and bucked only slightly;

then he bumped against the tree, and so stopped altogether. I remained in the saddle and pressed my heels into his flanks. He became restless; but by now he realized that there was nothing to be afraid of, so I removed the blindfold. He looked about him. Still in the saddle, I spoke to him, patted him, reassured him.

Next I had to discover whether or not he was suitable for riding. From the first day I had been tapping him gently on the rump with a switch, to accustom him to this signal. One day I mounted him, and winked to a boy nearby to untie him. The horse stood still, having no idea of what was expected of him. I tapped him with the switch—nothing doing. Then he got a good sharp blow, and lo! he started off. I kept him under control, out on the prairie, where he could run freely. He ran, and even galloped, but I kept holding him back more and more, until he realized that this was a signal to stop or fall into a different gait. Through all this time of training, I managed to keep my patience, never to break his pride; and so this strong, shaggy three-year-old became a good horse. I called him Gitano, which means gypsy.

Whether in the long history of mankind a colt had ever been trained for riding in a similar way, I don't know. Anyhow, the way I had done it produced lasting results, so my training system cannot have been so very wrong.

And now the herd had to be cut out. I possessed not the slightest notion what was meant by that and how it had to be done. Never in my life had I driven even as few as fifty cattle from one pasture to the next. Now, since Mr. Pratt was hawklike, watching every move I made preparing the herd for the long march, I was forced to show off here and there. If you wish you may call it shameless bluffing. Perhaps you are right. If I had never tried bluffing at some critical occasions in my existence on earth I would have lost my life long, long ago.

My idea (if it was good or wrong, this I did not know) was to form a little group of the animals into sort of a family center of the whole transport, around which smaller groups might gather and thus keep together more naturally, since cattle belong to the species of animals who for many good reasons prefer to live in groups or herds, as do dogs, horses, wolves, elephants, antelope, zebras—also fish.

Meantime, we had started cutting out the herd. First, I cut out the bulls, looking for a leader bull. We drove the bulls into the cattle corral I had picked, and I let them go hungry. I continued putting the herd, the two- and three-year-olds and the oxen, as well as the rest of the bulls, into another enclosure. I examined every one to make sure that it was healthy enough for the long trek; and all these were fenced into the field so that they might get the herd feeling. When I had three hundred head in that enclosure, I believed the bulls were ready.

We drove them into the field with the picked herd, and the battle for leader began. The bulls who were indifferent to the honor got themselves as far out of the way as possible, and the battle soon centered on five of them. The victor, still bleeding profusely, charged toward one of the cows in heat, who pushed her way toward him. We attended to all the wounded bulls immediately; and after the victor had spent himself and returned to his herd senses, he too got his medicine. For if the wounds weren't treated promptly, they'd soon be full of maggots, and it'd be a long and tedious job getting them out.

Worms, maggots, and ticks are a big problem with any herd, anywhere, but worst of all in the tropics. And if cattle start losing weight, their skin dries out, and deadens, and the lean cattle are in danger of being eaten alive by worms and ticks. Healthy animals, however, are attacked only by limited numbers of pests which can easily be kept under control.

Once we had cut out the thousand head of cattle, Mr. Pratt, a very generous man, gave me five extra healthy ones as replacements for those five in a thousand who were certain to fall sick or fail to survive the long drive.

Then I was given a hundred pesos cash in silver for transport expenses, besides some checks I could cash in case of emergency, and I was also given the delivery note to the terminal pasture. Then Mr. Pratt handed me a map.

The less said about this map, the better. You can put anything you like upon a map: roads, rivers, villages, towns, grasslands, water pools, mountain passes, and plenty more. Paper is patient; it won't refuse anything. But, though a river or a bridge appears on a map, it doesn't mean that you're going to find it where it is supposed to be.

It was a real joy to hear Mrs. Pratt swearing; every other word was "son-of-a-bitch," "bastard," or "f———ing," and more in the same beautiful strain. On a rancho like theirs, it could be damned lonely, and the nights were long, so you couldn't blame her for living her life as intensely as existence on a cattle rancho permitted. How else was the poor woman to use up the surplus energy, which, had she lived in a village or town, would have gone into chatting and gossiping with the neighbors all day? To her, everything was son-of-a-bitch; her husband, I, the Indians, the fly that dropped into her coffee cup, the Indian girl in the kitchen, her finger that she cut, the hen that fluttered on the table and upset the soup pot, her horse that moved too slowly—yes, every object between heaven and earth was to Mrs. Pratt a son-of-a-bitch.

They had a phonograph and we danced nearly every evening. For a number of reasons, I preferred to dance with the Indian kitchen maid; but Ethel, Mrs. Pratt, danced far better, and we got onto such good terms that one night she told me quite frankly in her husband's presence that she'd like to marry me if her husband should die or divorce her.

She was a fine woman, Mrs. Pratt, she certainly was, and I

wouldn't hear a word against her. A woman who can handle the wildest horse, swear to make a sergeant major wince, a woman before whom tough vaqueros trembled and with whom bandits kept their distance, a woman who in the presence of her husband (whom she seemed to love) could quite soberly declare that she'd like to marry.me if he died or left her—damn it, a woman like that could stir you even if you didn't care much about the so-called weaker sex.

As we were leaving, Ethel Pratt stood on the long veranda and waved good-bye. "Good luck, boy! You're always welcome on this rancho. Hey, Suarez, you dirty dog, you filthy son-of-a-goddamned-old-bitch, can't you see that black one is breaking out? Where are your f——ing eyes? Well, boy, good-bye!"

I waved my hat, and Gitano swept off with me.

23

 Yes, we were off. We broke out. The yelling, the shouting, the calling, the high-pitched shrieking of the Indians; the sound of the short-handled whips cutting through the air; the trampling of hoofs and all the uproar as a column of beasts shied off, rushed away, and had to be blocked in, lest it lost contact with the main herd.

The first day is always one of the hardest, so Mr. Pratt came along with us. The herd is still only loosely knit, and a sense of belonging together does not develop until the transport has been underway a few days, until the herd knows the leader bull and gets the smell of mutual kinship. Then the family feeling, rather the herd feeling, emerges and the animals want to stay with their herd.

But they didn't stay together like a flock of sheep kept in order by a shepherd and a dog. For these cattle, born and raised on vast ranges among Mr. Pratt's twelve-thousand-headed herd, were accustomed to space, and they wanted to spread out, run loose. The dogs we took with us couldn't make much of a showing, for they tired easily and could be used only for small jobs. Thus it was a constant galloping back and forth, shouting and yelling.

I had a police whistle with me as a signal for the boys; the foreman had an ordinary whistle, easily distinguished from mine. I put the foreman at the head and I took the rear, as it afforded a better view of the field of transport, and it seemed easier to me to direct operations from there.

What more beautiful sight could there be than a giant herd of healthy half-wild cattle! There they were ahead of me, trampling and stamping—the heavy necks, the rounded bodies, the proud, mighty horns. It was a heaving sea of gigantic vitality, of brute nature herded along by one single purpose. And each pair of horns represented a life in itself, a life with its own will, its own desires, its own thoughts and feelings.

From saddle-height I surveyed the whole of this ocean of horns and necks and rumps. I could perhaps have walked on the broad backs of the animals across the entire herd up to the belled bulls in front.

The animals bellowed singly and in chorus. They quarreled and pushed each other around. Shouts and calls went up. The bells clattered. The sun smiled and blazed. Everything was green—the land of perpetual summer. Oh, beautiful, wonderful land of everlasting springtime, rich with legend, dance, and song! You have no equal anywhere on this earth.

I couldn't help singing. I sang whatever came into my head, hymns and sweet folk airs, love songs and ditties, operatic arias, drinking songs and bawdy songs. What did I care what the songs were about? What did the melody matter? I sang from a heart full of joy.

And what magic air! The hot breath of the tropical bush, the warm, sultry sweat of the mass of moving cattle, the heavy vapors from a nearby swamp wafted to us by the wind.

Thick droves of buzzing horseflies and other insects circled over the trotting herd, and dense clouds of glittering green flies followed us to settle on the dung. Blackbirds accompanied us in whole flocks, lighted on the backs of the beasts to pick ticks and bugs from their hides. Untold thousands of creatures lived off this mighty herd. Life and life! Everywhere nothing but life.

Our march took us over country roads for a few days, with fields and pastureland on either side fenced in with barbed wire. Of course such pastures can't be used without the owner's consent, so our herd had to graze along the roadsides, which proved to be ample, and there were sufficient water pools still full from the rainy season.

When cars or trucks or pack caravans passed along the roads there was quite some performance, for we had to push the herd to one side; but the cattle would break away, wheel around, and hightail it singly or in groups for several miles. Then we'd have to give chase and round them up, drive them into the herd again.

It was even more complicated when we came to open pastures where other cattle were grazing in herds, often without herders. Sometimes these herds mixed in with ours and had to be sorted out; on one occasion this took practically a whole day, for we couldn't drive off a single head of another rancher's cattle. Had we done so, it would have led to unholy difficulties for which I, and in the last resort Mr. Pratt, would have been held responsible.

Sometimes, we couldn't get rid of straying animals. They insisted on following us, because they took a liking to our bulls perhaps, or liked the smell of our herd. I was always supposed to know at a glance if a stray animal got in with our herd, or one of ours lagged behind; but the brands and markings were often very similar and almost illegible. The foreman with an Indian driver was supposed to chase other herds away before our herd approached them; but it often happened that a few dozen head of our own would manage to scamper off with the other herd. Then the mix-up would be hell on hoofs, and we'd be soaked with sweat and have throats like sandpaper before we got them all sorted out again.

For a general to take an army overland is child's play compared with the task of transporting a thousand head of half-wild range cattle across undeveloped, half-primitive country. Soldiers can be told what's expected of them. Herds of cattle cannot; you have to do everything yourself. You are the superior and the subordinate in one.

At around five in the afternoon we usually called a halt, depending on whether we'd reached grazing land and water. The animals could hold out without water for one day provided they had fresh grass; two days, if they had to; but on the third day water had to be found. If I couldn't find water, I'd often let the herd run freely and they'd find it by themselves; but such water might be so far off our main line of advance that we'd lose a day or so.

We set up two camps at night, one in front and one in the rear. Fires were lighted, coffee made, beans or rice cooked, camp bread was baked, and dried meat eaten with it. Then we wrapped ourselves in our blankets and slept on the bare ground, with the sky for cover, our heads upon our saddles.

I posted two watches, with reliefs, to keep jaguars away and to keep the herd together. There are cattle who like to nose around at night just as some men do; and of course all the animals are up long before dawn, grazing. We gave them plenty of time for this, as well as a long rest at high noon.

After several days I had lost only one bull. He had been fighting and got so badly gored that we had to slaughter him. We cut out the best meat, sliced it thinly, and dried it in the broiling hot sun. To make up the loss of this one bull, a cow had calved the night before, and this presented us with a new problem. The little calf couldn't make the trek, but we didn't want to kill it. We wanted him to keep his noisy young life, and we felt sorry for the mother cow who licked her baby so lovingly. So I took the calf first on my own horse, then passed it to other riders about every half hour.

This little calf became our pet. He was a joy, and it was ever a touching sight when we handed him down to his mother, who always ran near the rider holding her calf. There was always a great licking, mooing and lowing at these reunions, where the little calf went at her udder and she was almost beside herself with joy. When he got heavier we had to load him onto a pack mule.

If too many cows had calved, it would have been impossible to show the mothers this consideration; but it happened three times more and I could never bring myself to kill the little ones.

Ingratitude is so much a part of human character that it is best to take it for granted and not feel hurt by it. Nature on the other hand is grateful for the smallest services we render her. No plant or animal ever forgets the drink of water it receives at our hands, or the handful of fodder that we may give it. And so did the little calves and their mothers, although unknowingly, present their gratitude to us for the charity we had shown them.

We came to a large river and neither we nor the guide could discover a ford. Farther downstream we found a ferry, but the ferryman demanded so much a head that the crossing would have been too costly; and I had yet to face the cost of other rivers, ferries, and toll bridges that had to be used, regardless. While I was bargaining with the ferryman, the herd rushed on upstream for another three miles. Here we stopped for two days, because the grazing was very good. Here they bathed, standing in the water for hours on end, ridding themselves of the various vermin that perished in water.

After two days of rest, we still had to cross the river. We started to drive them over, but as soon as they felt the incline

of the river bed, they turned back; though the river wasn't
very wide, there were deep channels.

At last I hit on an idea. Taking our machetes, we chopped
down some small trees and made a raft. We tied the lassos into
one long line and an Indian swam across with one end of the
line. We tied the other end to the raft, as well as a second
lighter line for pulling it back. I packed one of the calves onto
the raft, and the Indian pulled it over and landed the calf. We
pulled the raft back and sent a second calf over. In a few
minutes we had all four calves on the other side.

They stood over there alone, pathetically wobbling on their
spindly high legs, and set up a chorus of wretched mooing. It
sounded pitiful. And if the mooing of those small, helpless
creatures went straight to our hearts, how much more did it
affect the mothers. The little ones had cried out only a few
times when one of the mothers took to the water and swam
across. Soon, the other three mothers followed. There was an
affectionate reunion, but we hadn't time to watch it for much
hard work awaited us.

Now the mother cows were mooing, because they were
separated from the herd; they were afraid, and longed to be
reunited with their kith and kin. The bulls listened to the
mooing for a while and then began to swim over. The leader
bull was not among them. Only younger bulls had crossed
over, probably thinking they now had a chance to found a
new empire on the other side, away from any interference
from the older bulls. The jealousy of the older, bigger bulls
was thus aroused, including the leader bull's. They snorted, and
rushed over to teach those precocious young greenhorns a
lesson.

The water cooled them down, however, and by the time
they got to the other side they lost the urge to fight, although
they had been snorting so fiercely from the opposite bank.
Now that the bulls were over, the cows had no intention of

spending the rest of their lives with no bulls around; as they were in the habit of following the bulls everywhere, they followed them now. Soon the water was full of snorting, splashing cattle doing their best to swim across. It was a fine confusion of horned heads and of thrusting, monstrous backs.

When the going got perilous, some of them turned back, and this was the moment when we had to take a hand. If we let the timid ones turn back, half the herd might follow; they were all fighting, unable to keep a straight course in the swift water, and milling about and heading for any bank. So we went in with our horses, shouting, using our whips, heading them all across, across, and across to the other side. Three of them swam too far downstream, drifted out of our reach, and were swept away, lost to us.

These three were the sum total of our losses at this crossing. It was cheap at the price, for they weren't much good anyway; they'd made trouble on the transport, they were slackers, and the fewer slackers in any troop, the better. Now we let the herd have a good rest while we made camp for the night. That night one of my two-year-olds was killed by a jaguar, though none of us heard a sound of it. The carcass and paw marks told us the story next morning.

In every respect, I got off lightly. Crossing by means of the small ferry would have taken a week, and would have cost hundreds of pesos; and even at that, I'd have suffered losses. Cattle might have jumped off the ferry, or fallen victim to more jaguars or alligators had we stayed so long by the river. Thus, the pesos I saved went toward my earnings and bonus.

What I had saved at this river crossing, I owed to my dear little calves. The love we had shown to them and their mothers had been bountifully repaid.

24

  The cattle drive would not have seemed the real thing without bandits or rustlers. In fact, as each day passes, you feel rather surprised if they don't show up. A big cattle transport like ours can't take place in a vacuum. Dozens of men see it, it gets talked about, and you never know what pair of eyes is a scout for a band of cattle thieves or bandits.

One morning we met them. They came riding along quite innocently and might have been taken for ranch hands riding to market or looking for work. They approached from our flank.

"Hello!" called the leader. "Any tequila?"

"No," said I, "no tequila. But we've got some tobacco. You can have some."

"All right. We'll take it. Got any maize leaves?"

"We can spare two dozen."

"We'll take them too. Well, now, what about money? The transport must have money for ferries and toll bridges."

Things were getting hot—money. "We've no money with us, only checks."

"Checks, rubbish. Can't read."

They talked among themselves, and then the spokesman came riding alongside. "About the money, we'll look into that."

He searched my pockets, the saddlebags, saddle, and gear—no money. He found only the checks, and had to admit that I spoke the truth.

"We could do with some cows," he decided.

"I could do with some myself," I said. "I'm not the owner. I'm only in charge of transporting these cattle."

"Then you won't be hurt if I take out one or two for myself."

"Go ahead," I agreed, "help yourself. I've one good cow, but with a lame foot. She'll be in milk in three months. You can cure the hoof; it's not bad."

"Where is she?"

I had her driven out, and he liked her. All this time, the transport had been moving on, for it couldn't be halted by a word of command, like an army, particularly since there was no grazing. The rustlers obligingly rode along beside me.

The leader said: "Well, you've given me one, and now it's my turn to pick one out for myself."

He picked one, but he didn't know much about cattle, and I didn't mind losing the one he picked.

"Now you can pick one out for me," he granted.

I did so. Then he picked himself another one. This time he took one of the milk cows.

"Now it's your turn again, señor!" he called.

I had to have my little joke. I called the man who was carrying the milk cow's calf on his saddle. "Here you are, the little one in the bargain," I said, handing the little calf over to him. He was well satisfied with the bargain, and let the calf pass for a fully grown animal. But he wasn't acting out of generosity. Oh, no. Many people can't milk cows; or they can milk the cow only if the calf is sucking. The milk must practically flow by itself, as if she's giving the milk to her calf. So, the calf was a welcome gift to that man. He could now get milk from the cow for his family, or for sale.

It was his turn to pick out another cow.

When they rode away, they had seven cows and one calf—which cost me a hundred and seventy-five pesos. Of course, the possibility of bandits was duly considered when I made the contract with Mr. Pratt; it was only a question of how I'd deal with the bandits. It's best to bargain with them, as with businessmen, and employ diplomacy, too, for they might well have driven off with fifteen, instead of seven and a half.

It all counts up as business expense, like freight demurrage. It was a business risk, such as a derailed train, a ship wrecked or burned would be. In this country, at that time, no rancher insured his herd; no insurance company would issue a policy except at impossible rates. Bandits were a business risk, just as depot, freight, feeding, watering, taxing, and licensing might be in other regions. Here, the risks are rivers, mountains, mountain passes, gorges, sandy regions, waterless routes, bandits, jaguars, rattlesnakes, copperheads, and, if worst comes to worst, a cattle epidemic which might be caught from contact with other cattle met on the march.

Here, the cost was borne by the vastness of everything: the land, the herds, the breeding, the increase. Mr. Pratt's twelve thousand head were not among the largest herds of the region. Bandits and rustlers were just another factor. Of course, one can shoot at bandits, or threaten to call the military. Some fools may do that. You can always see it done, very nicely, in films: three dozen bandits fleeing from one smart cowboy. In the movies, yes; in reality, no. In reality, it's quite, but quite, quite different.

In reality, bandits do not gallop off so easily. It is the birthright of bandits to take what they need. Three hundred years of slavery and subjugation under Spanish overlords and

Church domination and torturers couldn't but demoralize the most upright people on earth. My bandits were pleased that they got everything so easily, so pleasantly, with such genial conversation, including my little calf joke. So we all were pleased.

Now we had to make a long detour, for a biggish town lay on our route, and no grazing ground near it. We had to make our way up a river cut, and then cross a range of mountains, la Sierra.

Here, it was getting cool. There was plenty of water about, but grazing was getting tight and the animals were eating leaves from the trees. Tree foliage was as filling as grass, and seemed to make a pleasant change for the cattle. As I watched them stripping the leaves off trees so neatly I couldn't but believe that cattle in ancient times may not have been prairie and steppe beasts, but beasts of the forest, living off shrubs and low-branched trees, in woods that have nearly disappeared while tall high-growing trees have survived.

The mountain crossing was laborious, for these range cattle were not used to mountain trails. Two lost their footholds, one of them a magnificent young bull. He went down with his cow just as they were merrily copulating—a tragedy of love. We could see them lying in the gorge below, smashed. For all that, I'd anticipated more falls.

We had two cases of snakebite, too. One morning we noticed that two of the cows had swollen legs; examination showed the fang marks. But the cows had been lucky, evidently not fatally infected with the venom. We treated the wounds by cutting them open, bathing them in pure alcohol, and applying tourniquets above the wound. We had a two-day halt, once that crossing was behind us, and the cows picked up well. I was glad to be able to save them.

That evening two Indians started a terrible argument as to

what kind of snakes those had been. One maintained for rattle-snakes; the other insisted on copperheads. I settled the dispute, which threatened to become serious, by drawing a parallel: "Castillo, if you were shot at, or worse, shot dead, it wouldn't matter to you whether you were shot with a revolver or a rifle, would it?"

"Seguro, señor, this doesn't matter. Shot is shot."

"There you are, muchachos. The same goes for cows. They've been bitten by poisonous snakes, by rattlers or coppers. It hurts. As for the rest, they don't give a damn."

"You're right, señor, a poisonous snake. Who cares what kind?"

They found my dictum so clever that they turned from snakes to curability of snakebites, discussing all kinds of herbs and Indian remedies, and so their quarrel petered out.

25

  One day at sunrise when we were calling the signal to start off, I rode up a hill to see beyond the herd and decide on our direction. From the hilltop, I could see church spires in the distance.

Laid about with dawn's shimmering gold, the end was in sight!

Our troubles were over. In that town over there, bathed in golden sunlight, joy awaited us. I left the herd on the prairie, ordered camp pitched, galloped into town and wired Mr. Pratt. It was evening when I got back to camp, where the fires were blazing and the two vaqueros on guard watch were riding leisurely about singing the animals to sleep.

To man, who has always been a diurnal creature, there is something indescribably uncanny about the tropic night; and tropic nights are also uncanny to diurnal animals. In the evenings, small herds gather round the rancho house to be near man, knowing that man is their protector. During the weeks after the rainy season when mosquitoes and horseflies zoom through the air, thick as swirling dust, the cattle come home from the prairies to congregate around the rancho house, expecting help. But you can't help them because you've

194

wrapped your own face and hands in cloth to protect yourself against the evil spirits of the tropical hell.

Even great herds on their home ranches get restless at sundown. They surround the huts of the vaqueros, and the watches ride around them, singing, throughout the night, and the animals lie down to sleep. Some of the big breeders leave it to the vaqueros to sing or not, for some think it's unnecessary. But cattle not sung to sleep are restless the whole night through, lying down for ten minutes, then getting up to prowl around and rub against the others for companionship. The cattle are then sleepy next day, and feed less than cattle sung to sleep, and hence take longer to fatten into shape. During transports, singing is even more essential, for cattle are even more restless, having to lie as they do on strange earth.

So I had my men sing every night, and they did it willingly. As the men rode slowly around them, singing, the cattle would lie down with a feeling of absolute security; drowsily the cattle would follow the singing rider with their eyes, moo and low, sigh gigantically, and settle to sleep. The more singing through the night, the better, for the cattle felt reassured that nothing could happen to them, as man was near to shield them from all dangers, including jaguars and mountain lions. I might add that my own kind of cowboy singing would keep away anyone who adored music. My own singing, for instance, was regarded as the eighth wonder of the world, but not as music.

A front watch was no longer necessary, as the river guarded us, and the flanks needed only the two regular watches. I took the foreman from the front, so we could all spend the last evenings together. Later, while the men smoked and chatted around the big fire, I saddled up and rode watch along the herd, singing, whistling, humming, calling to the cattle.

Clear as only the tropic night can be, the blue-black sky arched over the singing prairie along the river. The glittering stars studded the velvet night with gold. Dozens of falling stars streaked the heavens, as if winging from the high lonely dome in search of love or to give love, so unobtainable in those lonely heights where no bridge spans the void from one star to the other.

On the grassy flats, only glowworms and fireflies were visible. But invisible life sang with a million voices and made music like that of violin, flute, and harp—and tiny cymbal, and bell.

There lay my herd! One dark, rounded form next to the other. Lowing, breathing, exhaling a full, warm, heavy fragrance of natural well-being, so rich in its quiet earthiness, such balm to the spirit, bringing with it such utter contentment.

My army! My proud army which I'd led over river and mountain, which I'd protected and guarded, which I'd fed and watered, whose quarrels I'd settled and whose ills I'd cured, which I'd sung to sleep night after night, for which I'd grieved and worried, for whose safety I'd trembled, and whose care had robbed me of sleep, for which I'd wept when one was lost, which I'd loved and loved, yes, loved as if it had been of my own flesh and blood!

Oh, you who took armies of warriors over the Alps to carry murder and pillage into lands of peace, what do you know of the joy, the perfect joy, of leading an army!

The next morning the salt transport came out. I'd given them salt only once during the whole march; for it's not wise to risk salting unless you've plenty of water for them the same day, and the next. Now, however, they took salt and drank water to their fill, so they took on such a magnificent plump appearance, like soldiers with new uniforms. Their hides, well-rubbed, gleamed as if lacquered. Yes, I was proud of my transported herd.

In a few days, Mr. Pratt arrived with his cattle agent.

"Damn it all, man," the agent kept saying, "that's some cattle. They'll sell like hotcakes in cold season."

Mr. Pratt kept shaking my hand. "Boy oh boy, how did you do it? I didn't expect you until the end of next week. I've already sold four hundred head. There's another breeder on the way, and if you'd have been late, the price would have been lower, for this market can't take two thousand head in one week. Come on, I'll drive you into town. The foreman can manage the herd now."

In town, we settled accounts, and I had hundreds of pesos in hand. Still, he stood me to a real dinner.

"If I get a good price," said Mr. Pratt, "I'll give you another hundred pesos as an extra bonus. You've earned it. You got off lightly with those damned bandits."

"I must tell you, honestly," I admitted, "one of the bandits I knew personally, a certain Antonio. Once I picked cotton with him. He saw to it that I got off lightly."

"That's just the point. You must have good luck—everywhere, whether you breed cattle, drive them, or take a wife." He burst out laughing. "Tell me, boy, what did you do to my wife?"

"Me? To your wife?" The food stuck in my mouth, and I thought I turned pale. Women! They can act so irresponsibly! They get all sorts of notions into their heads; out of the blue, they may get a confession jag. Could she possibly have spilled the beans? She didn't seem the type.

"When your wire arrived, she really raved. 'There you are! See what a wash-out you are! A dead loss. But that boy gets the herd over, as if he was carrying it in a hamper slung on his pommel. Just like you couldn't ever do. This fellow's got something, the f———ing son-of-a-bitch!' "

"For goodness' sake, Mr. Pratt, you're not thinking of divorce?"

"Divorce? Me? Whatever for? Because of a trifle like that?"

He gave me an odd smile. If only I knew what it meant. "No. Why should I get a divorce? Are you afraid I might?"

"Yes," I confessed.

"But why?"

"Because your wife said she'd marry me."

"Oh. Yes, I remember her saying that, and if she says she's going to do a thing, she does it. But why are you squirming like that? Scared? Don't you like my wife? I thought that—"

I didn't let him finish that one. "I like your wife very much," I confessed rapidly. "But—please don't get a divorce! If I did marry her, it wouldn't be a bad thing, perhaps, but I really don't know what I'd do with a wife, I beg your pardon, what I should do with your wife."

"What you'd do with any woman! Give her what she likes."

"That's not the point. It's something else. I don't know how I'd get on as a married man." I tried hard to make it clear to him. "Understand, I'm only a vagabond. I'm incapable of staying put on my rear. I couldn't drag my wife along on my travels; nor could I stay put, and sit at a proper table with a proper breakfast and a proper dinner every day. No! My stomach wouldn't stand it, either. Now, if you'd like to do me a favor——"

"Anything you like. Granted," he said good-naturedly.

"Don't divorce your wife. She's such a good wife, such a beautiful, clever, brave wife! You'd never get another like her, Mr. Pratt."

"I know that. That's why I wouldn't get a divorce. I never thought of such a thing. I don't know how you got such nonsense into your head! Come off that, now, and we'll go celebrate the end of your cattle contract."

And off we went.

Mr. Pratt abruptly stopped drinking. Now what is he going to do to me? I thought to myself. Shoot or what?

"Yes, Mr. Pratt," I stammered, "what's up now?"

"What do you think happened while you were away with the cattle?"

"What? Mr. Pratt, I'm all ears." I felt so confused that I had to search for words.

"La Aurora Bakery," he said, dryly.

"Yes, yes, come on, what happened to the good old Aurora?"

"The bakers are on strike, and apparently no end of it in sight."

"On strike, the bakers of La Aurora?"

"Yes, but not only of La Aurora. All the bakeries of the port are on strike. Not a bite of bread can be bought, not even a stale roll. The're all eating tortillas. I've never seen so many women selling tortillas."

"Too bad," I said.

"And do you know what the Douxs are telling the whole world?"

"No, what?"

"That you started that bakers' strike."

"I? Me? So help me, how could I do such a thing? Me, driving a herd of cattle cross country? The bakers out on strike and I so many miles away? So here you can see clearly what sort of rotten slanderers the Douxs are—unjust through and through. I know nothing whatsoever about this bakers' strike."

"Listen. The Douxs are saying that since the time you came to work there, the bakehouse men have been dissatisfied with everything—with the food, sleeping quarters, wages, and with the long hours. You'd hardly left the place when things got going. Then, strike! One day it was La Aurora, next day all the bakeries were struck. The men now want two pesos a day, better food and better sleeping quarters, and an eight-hour day."

"Well, now I'll tell you the honest truth, Mr. Pratt. Honestly, I had nothing to do with that strike. I told you this the first time we met, when you told me what Shine had said about me, that—by pure chance!—a strike always broke out where I was working or where I had been working, even if I'd hardly had time to look around me. Well, I can't help that. It's not my fault if men get dissatisfied and want something better. I never say anything to such men. I keep mum, and let others do the talking. So it beats me, everywhere I go people say I'm a Wobbly, a troublemaker, and I assure you, Mr. Pratt, that this is——"

"The whole and unadulterated truth," Mr. Pratt finished the sentence that I'd intended to finish quite differently.

That's how it goes, if people take the words out of your mouth and twist them around. Really, it's no wonder that people get the wrong impression about all matters and things.

People should let a fellow have his say. But no, they must always interfere in another person's affairs. No wonder it doesn't make sense.